The Main VO Players in Order of

Ms. Kirby Shirrah - U.S. President

Collette Smythe - Presidential Secretary

Bob Maxwell - Secretary of Defense

Elaine Kellog - Presidents Science Advisor

Colonel Sanji Batii - White House Intelligence Liaison Officer

Carol Barr - Lead Oceanographer - Atlas II

Beth Spall - Oceanographer - Atlas II

Robert Carlisle - Oceanographer - Atlas II

Mary Osterwald - Director Homeland Security

Admiral Jack Tullie - Commander Naval Task Force

VO

Bell Carroll - Secretary of State

Admiral Walter Ripleton - Director Naval Intelligence

Captain Tug Bradley - Carrier Pilot

Jane Colucci - Marine Biologist

Benjamin Darius - Director NASA

Odette Hume - Theoretical Physicist

William Duggin - BBC Director General

Laynie Val - White House Communications

Liza Newborn - NSA

Maria Cole - Director NEO

Jay Parkeshmushmundar - Co Director NEO

Ms. Cai Morwen - United Nations General Secretary

Linda Paul - Moon Mission Commander

Joel Krause - Moon Mission Mechanical Engineer

Svetlana Koblikov - Moon Mission Russian Specialist

Lakota Hightower - Moon Mission Cinematographer

FADE IN:

INT. PRESIDENT'S OFFICE - 9:00 AM   1

Humming softly to herself and making notes for the days meetings, the President, **KIRBY SHIRRAH**, sits at her desk, unaware of the excitement soon to occur. **COLLETTE SMYTHE,** the president's secretary is seated nearby shuffling through documents. A busy day planned but so far unremarkable. Sitting relaxed, listening to a classical radio station when, suddenly, the B-52s song CHANNEL Z plays. They exchange perplexed looks. Collette shrugs her shoulders and both go back to their respective activities while humming along.

Simultaneously we see a montage of civilians and military who are picking up the song on their headsets, cell phones, computers, hearing aids, televisions, everything, everywhere.

As the classical program resumes, the phone rings and is picked up by the President.

                    KIRBY
          (cheerfully)
     Hello ?

                    SECRETARY OF DEFENSE (V.O.)
     Madam President, could you please
     join us in the situation room ASAP.

                    KIRBY
     I take it we are having a
     situation Bob.

                    SECRETARY OF DEFENSE (V.O.)
     Yes ma'am.

                    KIRBY
          (big sigh)
     I'll be right over.

2 INT. SITUATION ROOM - 20 MINUTES LATER   2

The President walks into the situation room. Seated are the Joint Chiefs, Secretary of Defense **BOB MAXWELL,** the President's Science Adviser **ELAINE KELLOG** and a very agitated full bird Colonel, **SANJI BATII,** White House Intelligence Liaison Officer.

Kirby does not immediately take charge of the meeting,
preferring to let everyone get organized, a cup of
coffee and a deep breath. She does, however, go
straight for the doughnuts and this group knows better
than to get between the leader of the free world and
the pastry plate. Bob Maxwell starts off.

                         BOB
               Madam President, ladies and
               gentlemen, we have an interesting
               situation.

                         SANJI
               Don't sugar coat it Bob. We have
               just experienced a total intrusion
               into the civilian and military
               communications systems worldwide.

                         KIRBY
               Details Colonel, I get cranky when
               I miss my Red Bull break and
               doughnuts only go so far.

The room erupts in laughter. They are all used to
Kirby's disarming manner by now but she always manages
to surprise. Colonel Batii is becoming increasingly
anxious at this point and motions for quiet.

                         SANJI
               With all due deference Madam
               President, this is no laughing
               matter. For exactly four minutes
               and twenty seconds this morning, a
               rock and roll song played out of
               every communications system on
               Earth. satellite, radio and
               television were all effected,
               including all of our encrypted
               networks.

                         KIRBY
               That explains what Collette and I
               heard on NPR this morning. We
               thought it was a little odd, even
               for a pledge drive.

A generalized chuckle spreads throughout the group

                         BOB
               Better give Sanji a break chief
               before he strokes out.

Kirby throws her hands up.

> KIRBY
> Okay Bob, you win. Do we know
> anything at all ?

Colonel Batii uses a pointer to show a spot on the
world map in the Pacific ocean.

> SANJI
> We **think** it originated in this
> area of the Pacific near Guam.

> KIRBY
> We **think** ?

> SANJI
> At a depth of approximately thirty
> eight thousand feet.

A round of interesting comments circulates through the
room. Oh my God, somebody was drunk on duty, not
possible and the ever popular, must be aliens. No one
knew how close to the mark that last one really was.

> ELAINE
> Colonel, do we or anyone else have
> any transmission equipment that
> powerful ?

Bob Maxwell raises his hand.

> BOB
> I got this one. We do have VLF
> gear. It's used to communicate
> with our submarines that have
> dived deep. Theoretically, it will
> go all the way around the Earth
> but not at power levels that would
> high jack the planet or on all
> these different frequencies.

> KIRBY
> Do we think its a prelude to
> something nasty or just a high
> tech prank of some kind.

Bob's expression changes to furrowed brow serious and
the group quiets down. Bob looks directly at the
President.

                              BOB
                  We think it should be treated as
                  hostile until **we** know it isn't.

                              KIRBY (SMILING)
                  Don't be snotty Bob. Are there any
                  specific suggestions on what
                  resources we should prioritize ?

Admiral **KELLY** rises and turns to face Kirby.

                              KELLY
                  Madam President, it would be
                  prudent to get a task force moving
                  in that direction. We have the
                  best mobile underwater detection
                  and satellite gear. If it happens
                  again, we'll be right on top of it.

Kirby, to the entire group.

                              KIRBY
                  Alright Admiral, proceed. Colonel
                  Batii will coordinate all of our
                  intelligence efforts from here.

As the meeting breaks up, Kirby yells after everyone.

                              KIRBY
                  I want regular updates people.

3 EXT. MARIANAS NEAR CHALLENGER DEEP - 2 HOURS EARLIER

The deep ocean, beautiful, mysterious, foreboding.
Lethal to the human physical state and only accessed
with specially constructed craft. An R.O.V., gleaming,
brightly lit, glides effortlessly through the
colorless depths. Operated from the research ship
Atlas 2 on site in the Marianas, it touches down in
this unfamiliar realm. Researchers aboard ship begin
the task of cataloging the sea life.

Amid the high tech clutter of computers and remote
monitors, expedition leader **CAROL BARR** is watching the
R.O.V. camera feed.

                              CAROL
                  Hey guys, do you see what I see ?

Fellow team members **BETH SPALL** and **ROBERT CARLISLE**
come over for a look.

Beth walks over and squints at Carol's screen.

                    BETH
          You mean that glow to the left ?

Carol is wide eyed, unblinking and hardly breathing.

                    CAROL
          Yeah.

                    ROBERT
          It comes and goes. Luminescent
          fish ?

                    CAROL
          Awfully bright for a fish.

Working the R.O.V.s' control stick, Carol gently
nudges the platform left and almost immediately bumps
into something really, really big. Looming close up in
the remote camera lens is a wall. Glowing pale silver,
composed of 6 sided polygons with pulsing centers,
like an impossibly gigantic chicken wire cage.

                    CAROL
               (ecstatic)
          Where's the sat phone, I gotta
          call Woods Hole !

Robert searches frantically for a handset.

                    ROBERT
          Woods Hole hell, call NASA

                    BETH
          I've got to see how big this thing
          is. I'm bringing the remote up.

Beth hurriedly takes over the joystick, the robot
jerks and twists.

                    ROBERT
               (Chiding)
          Beth, slow it down, we can't
          afford to lose the camera.

                    BETH
          I love you Robert but go push a
          button or something will ya, I'm a
          little busy.

                         CAROL
                    (teasing)
               Play nice boys and girls.

All eyes on the screen, intent on the overwhelming
size of the structure, as the remote rises through
twenty thousand feet...ten thousand feet...

                         CAROL (CONT'D)
               We are about to go down in
               history, I don't know what for yet
               but we are going to be **crazy**
               famous.

                         ROBERT
               Holy crap, this thing is **huge** ! I
               don't understand why it didn't
               show up on sonar ? Cameras coming
               up on two thousand feet.

                         CAROL
               Stop, stop. That's it, that's the
               top. Beth, take it along there,
               see how wide it is.

The submersible hovers silently over the top edge of
this mesmerizing structure. An assortment of sea life
glides effortlessly by, seemingly unperturbed. Some
are actually resting on the structure itself.

                         CAROL
               What's the count so far ?

Robert looks over the data

                         ROBERT
               We just hit another corner, 1,500
               feet !

Everyone is at a loss for words but finally...

                         CAROL
               Wow !

                         BETH
               Well, what now ?

                         CAROL
               Set the rover down on the wall and
               keep updating the GPS. We'll see
               if its moving.

                              BETH
                    Moving...what do you mean **moving** ?
                    Its seven miles high and 1,500
                    feet wide where's it gonna go ?

Robert chuckles and rolls his eyes at the suggestion.

                              CAROL
                    I don't know...I got excited, do
                    it anyway.

Robert has finally gotten a call through.

                              ROBERT
                    Hey Carol, I've got Woods Hole on
                    the line. What do you want to do ?

Carol pauses to think for a moment.

                              CAROL
                    Up link ! We need an up link for
                    the data and camera feeds !

Carol sits down, her head in her hands.

                              CAROL (CONT'D)
                    Coffee, I need large amounts of
                    coffee.

Beth bolts up and points at the computer display while
yelling to Carol.

                              BETH
                    Carol...Carol its moving. The
                    damned thing is actually moving.

                              CAROL
                    What direction ?

                              ROBERT
                    Its coming straight up. This is
                    incredible !

                              CAROL
                    Are we transmitting to Woods Hole ?

Robert double checks with the party on the phone.

                              ROBERT
                    They are getting it all and in
                    real time.....**now.**

Remote pictures from the submersible are becoming a jumbled blur.

> BETH
> I can't hold the remote on the wall, its coming up so fast, the turbulence is knocking it all over the place.

Rushing over to Beth.

> CAROL
> Try and keep it parallel, we can film it rising.

Beth quickly moves the remote out of the direct path of the structure and focuses the camera on one facet which is, apparently, motionless.

> BETH
> It looks stationary ? Could it be .....**growing** ?

> ROBERT
> Dunno but it **is** surfacing.

The ships Captain makes an urgent announcement.

> CAPTAIN (V.O.)
> Hey doc, you and your people better get topside. Something is breaking the surface to port, about one thousand yards.

Everyone trips over themselves trying to get on deck. Carol stops half way up the stairway...

> CAROL
> Oh crap, no camera, wait for me.

4 <u>INT. PRESIDENT'S OFFICE - SAME DAY</u>   4

Bob Maxwell enters the President's office and Kirby is on a speaker phone conference with **MARY OSTERWALD,** Director of Homeland Security and Colonel Batii who is now at NSA headquarters trying to confirm the signals exact origin.

> KIRBY
> Hang on folks, Bob Maxwell just walked in.

                              BOB
                    You're gonna love this chief. The
                    Navy just got a call from Woods
                    Hole Oceanographic, They are on a
                    live feed from a research ship in
                    the Pacific called Atlas 2. Their
                    rover found a glowing structure
                    1,500 feet on a side and seven
                    miles high in the Marianas trench
                    off Guam. It seems to be rising up
                    from the bottom of the trench.

Several seconds of stunned silence, slack jaws and
raised eyebrows, then Kirby gets on the intercom to
Elaine Kellog.

                              KIRBY
                    Elaine ?

                              ELAINE (V.O.)
                    Yes chief.

                              KIRBY
                    Get in here quick with your big
                    scientific brains list. We're
                    going to need help.

                              ELAINE (V.O.)
                    Do I get to know why ?

                              KIRBY
                    If you grab me a doughnut.

                              ELAINE (V.O.)
                    On my way chief.

Kirby turns back to her phone call.

                              KIRBY
                    You still on Mary ?

                              MARY (V.O.)
                    I'm with you chief, what would you
                    like to do alert wise ?

                              KIRBY
                    We don't know much of anything yet
                    so don't churn up the **whole** pond
                    but tell your people to stay sharp.

                        MARY (V.O.)
          No offense chief but that's a
          little vague.

                        KIRBY
          Assume you can act on the fly,
          I've got your back.

                        MARY (V.O.)
          Understood chief.

                        SANJI
          Ma'am.

                        KIRBY
          Go ahead Colonel.

                        SANJI
          We have arranged a parallel feed
          with Woods Hole and the Atlas 2.
          You should have live video now on
          monitor four.

Bob walks over to the video set-up and grabs the
remote.

                        BOB
          Hang on Sanji, we're working on it.

The monitor lights up and underwater footage from the
rover is split screen with an over the rail shot by
Carol Barr as the structure breaks the surface. Elaine
Kellog comes in.

                        ELAINE
          What did I miss ?

                        BOB
          Sssssssh.

An image presents, so incomprehensible, that except
for gasps of Oh My God, words completely fail.

5 EXT. PACIFIC OCEAN - NAVY TASK FORCE - SAME DAY   5

ADMIRAL JACK TULLIE is on the bridge of the Navy Task
Force 3 carrier CVN-77, the George H.W. Bush, en route
to rendezvous with Atlas 2. Tullie is reviewing his
coded orders from the Commander in Chief.

Read out loud by Admiral Tullie.

                    TULLIE
          To Commander Task Force 3 from
          Commander in Chief Washington -
          Provide all necessary technical
          assistance to research team on
          site - Establish cordon to deny
          site access by other vessels until
          further notice - Under no
          circumstances is force to be used
          without a direct order from the
          President - end. Well, that's
          clear enough.

The admiral requests communications with Atlas 2.

                    TULLIE (CONT"D)
          Lieutenent, see if you can get
          Doctor Barr on her sat phone.

                    COMMUNICATIONS OFFICER
          Aye sir. (Dialing)

On the Atlas 2, CAROL searches for her ringing phone.

                    CAROL (V.O.)
          Hello..hello..

                    COMMUNICATIONS OFFICER
          Doctor Barr, this is Navy CVN-77,
          Admiral Tullie calling, will you
          hold please.

                    CAROL (V.O.)
          Yes...of course.

                    TULLIE
          Hello Doctor, this is Admiral
          Tullie. At the request of the
          President, my naval group is on
          its way to assist your team.

                    CAROL (V.O.)
          Wow... I'll have to write the
          President a big thank you note.

                    TULLIE
          Our pleasure ma'am. We are still
          about 20 hours away, are there any
          new developments ? We... (CONT'd)

                         TULLIE (CONT'D)
                 don't have the video feed yet.

Carol looks out at the pristine ocean where the block
is hurling itself upward, yet creating not even a
ripple on the surface. Almost serene....almost.

                         CAROL
                 Admiral, I wish you were here.
                 It's rising at 10 feet a minute
                 and already 150 feet above sea
                 level. A gigantic polygon.

                         TULLIE
                 We have all the deep water
                 equipment we could get on short
                 notice but my orders are to give
                 you every possible assistance so
                 we'll scramble what ever is needed.

                         CAROL
                 I appreciate your help Admiral. I
                 wish I could tell you **what** we need
                 but I just haven't a clue yet.

                         TULLIE
                 See you soon DOCTOR (Clicks off)

6 <u>EXT. HIGH OVERHEAD VIEW - STRUCTURE AND TASK FORCE</u> 6

Ships sailing towards the rendezvous point and the
polygonal structure rising from the sea.

7 <u>INT. THE VO STRUCTURE - FOLLOWING DAY - AFTERNOON</u>   7

VO is five hundred feet in the air, at the top edge of
the structure, looking out at the Naval activity
through a large polygonal window. He watches Atlas 2
relaunching the R.O.V. and the two helicopters taking
off from the carrier. As VO observes, one of the
choppers passes directly in front of him.

                         VO (TO SELF)
                 Navy guys, time to say hi.

VO waves at the copter and startles the marine in the
doorway trying to film.

                         CAMERAMAN
                 Skipper...Did you see that ?

                        PILOT - CORAL 1
    See what ?

                        CAMERAMAN
    There's someone in there, he just
    waved at me !

                        PILOT - CORAL 1
    Did you record it ?

                        CAMERAMAN
    No, I got excited and missed the
    whole thing..

                        PILOT - CORAL 1
    Hang on, I'll come back around.
    CORAL 1 to CORAL 2 - over.

                        PILOT - CORAL 2 (V.O.)
    This is CORAL 2 - over.

                        PILOT _ CORAL 1
    Come back around and cover us. My
    spotter saw someone inside the
    structure - over.

                        PILOT - CORAL 2 (V.O.)
    Acknowledged CORAL 1 - out.

As CORAL 2 heads back, CORAL 1 swings around.

                        PILOT - CORAL 1
    Okay son, where do you want it ?

                        CAMERAMAN
    This facet skipper, up at the top
    center.

The chopper is once again right in front of VO and he
waves for the second time. CORAL 1 is hurriedly taking
pictures, CORAL 2 is close by, also filming.

                        VO (TO SELF)
    Hope he got my good side. Well,
    back to work.

VO walks away from the window and it takes on its
previous opaque and glowing state. VO reappears in the
ships great room surrounded by hundreds of video
screens, dials, gauges and floating T'AH.

                              CAMERAMAN
                    I got him clear skipper.

                              PILOT CORAL 1
                    CORAL 1 to base, mission
                    accomplished - over.

                              CARRIER (V.O.)
                    Acknowledged CORAL 1, return to
                    base - out.

7 INT. PRESIDENT'S OFFICE - NEXT MORNING

President Shirrah, Elaine Kellog, Bob Maxwell and the
Secretary of State **BELL CARROLL** are being briefed by
ADMIRAL WALTER RIPLETON the Director of Naval
Intelligence. They are about to see photos taken of
the structure and VO. All eyes on the monitor.

                              RIPLETON
                    These images were taken yesterday
                    in the Marianas. You can clearly
                    see a human...**ish** figure, inside
                    the structure, waving at the
                    chopper.

                              ELAINE
                    Did we make any attempts to
                    communicate Admiral ?

                              RIPLETON
                    No ma'am, the pilots instructions
                    were observe and photograph only.
                    Admiral Tullie decided to delay
                    further action until he could
                    consult with the intelligence
                    people and the Prresident.

                              KIRBY
                    Is the cordon in place Admiral ?

                              RIPLETON
                    Yes ma'am, the carrier group is
                    enforcing a twenty mile exclusion
                    zone for ships and a one hundred
                    mile no fly zone but once word
                    gets out, the consensus of opinion
                    is, that it will become impossible
                    to keep anyone out.

                          KIRBY
                     (To Bell Carroll)
               What do you think Bell ?

                          BELL
               Well, it's in international waters
               so we can't exactly plant a flag
               on it and apparently, the owner is
               home.

                          BOB
               You know chief, we could call it a
               safety zone. Tell everyone we are
               making sure there isn't harmful
               radiation or noxious chemicals or
               something. Just don't tell them
               it's inhabited before we have a
               chance to make contact.

                          KIRBY
               I'm not happy about stretching the
               truth for any reason but I see
               your point. What do you think
               Bell ?

                          BELL
               Works for me. Also, I'd rather the
               U.S. have the first conversation
               with whoever or whatever is in
               there, for our own general
               security if nothing else.

                          KIRBY
               We also need a little stall time
               for Elaine to gather up a science
               team and get them on site.

                          KIRBY (CONT'D)
               Alright folks, here's what I want
               to do, tell Admiral Tullie to go
               ahead and try communications but
               absolutely nothing aggressive. Is
               everybody clear on that point ?
               Bob, Walt ?

                          RIPLETON
               Afirmative.

                          BOB
               Understood chief.

                         KIRBY
          Elaine, start putting together a
          team. Any immediate thoughts ?

                         ELAINE
          Multidisciplinary. Medical,
          Biologic, engineering, materials,
          electronics and although no one
          has broached the subject yet, an
          astrophysicist or two. I mean, it
          could be from like...out there,
          couldn't it ?

                         KIRBY
          I was thinking Atlantis myself but
          on that subject, what happens if
          it is from...out there ? Bob ?

                         BOB
          Not sure chief. We'll have to play
          that one by ear. Call NASA I guess.

                         KIRBY
          Not an inspirational answer Bob.

                         BOB
          Sorry chief.

                         KIRBY
          Lets get going.

The meeting breaks up and everyone is energized by the
discovery. The President and Elaine are left alone for
a personal moment.

                         KIRBY
          I hope we don't screw this up
          Elaine.

                         ELAINE
          As long as we treat the situation
          as scientific discovery Kirby,
          It'll be fine. If it becomes
          military, well, we've screwed
          that up more than once.

                         KIRBY
          I'm not worried about us. I'm
          worried about the wider world. We
          don't have a monopoly on stupid.

                              ELAINE
                    True enough.

8 <u>INT. CARRIER CVN-77 - BRIEFING ROOM - DAY</u>

Admiral Tullie is on the phone with the President.

                              KIRBY (V.O.)
                    Good morning Admiral.

                              TULLIE
                    Madam President, good morning.

                              KIRBY (V.O.)
                    These orders are coming down
                    through channels Admiral but I
                    want to make certain we have no
                    unfortunate misunderstandings.

                              TULLIE
                    Affirmative.

                              KIRBY (V.O.)
                    I want you to defer all the
                    investigative decisions to Doctor
                    Barr for now and give her your
                    complete support. My science
                    adviser Elaine Kellog will
                    hopefully be joining you with
                    additional personnel and
                    equipment. Once Elaine is on site,
                    she will be in direct charge of
                    scientific operations. Clear ?

                              TULLIE
                    Clear.

                              KIRBY (V.O.)
                    Also, I know enforcing the cordon
                    is likely to get messy but its
                    imperative that we don't piss
                    anyone off if we can help it.

                              TULLIE
                    Understood. We are going to try
                    communications shortly.

                              KIRBY (V.O.)
                    Keep us up to date Admiral (Clicks
                    off)

Admiral Tullie joins his technical support staff.
LIEUTENANT RITA ERICSON reports.

                    ERICSON
          We're ready to start Admiral.

                    TULLIE
          Proceed Lieutenant.

                    ERICSON
          Initially sir, we considered a
          trial of commercial frequencies
          but I think its more to the point
          to find out if they are reading
          the encrypts.

                    TULLIE
          Agreed but try the commercial
          frequencies first. Let's not give
          them anything we don't have to.

                    ERICSON
          Aye sir.

The meeting is interrupted by the intercom.

                    INTERCOM (V.O.)
          Communications to Admiral Tullie.

                    TULLIE
          Tullie, go ahead.

                    INTERCOM (V.O.)
          Sir, you are getting a message.

                    TULLIE
          From where ?

                    INTERCOM (V.O.)
          Everywhere sir, every channel,
          every frequency, all at once.

                    TULLIE
          Record it, see if you can find the
          transmission point and put it
          through.

                    VO
               (cheerfully)
          Hi Jack, how's it hanging ?

                    TULLIE
               (surprised)
          Who am I speaking with please ?

                    VO (V.O.)
          Call me VO.

                    TULLIE
          May I ask where you are calling
          from Mr. VO.

                    VO (V.O.)
          I am inside what you have been
          calling **the structure**.

                    TULLIE
          And what do you call it sir ?

                    VO
               (Chuckles)
          Home.

                    TULLIE
          I hope we're not intruding sir.

                    VO
          Nah, I was expecting you. Oh, by
          the way, your submarines are here.

                    TULLIE
          How did you know that, may I ask ?

                    VO
          Embrace the mystery Jack.

                    TULLIE
          I'd like to meet with you, is that
          possible ?

                    VO (V.O.)
          Mmmmm, tell you what Jack, give me
          twenty minutes. (Clicks off)

                    TULLIE
          Com, get me the President.

9 INT. STRUCTURE - 1 HOUR LATER - DAY   9

VO is in a long room that is covered on all sides with
pulsing lights, polygonal view screens, ...(CONT'D)

gauges and his floating, puffy help, the T'AH. Face
on, VO is of general humanoid appearance, covered in
glowing polygons, black eyes, hairless, 7 fingers on
each hand, expressive, handsome, in an alien sort of
way. About six feet tall. Observing the activity above
and below the water, the task force ships, sea life
and submarines surrounding the structure appear to be
suspended in clear glass. VO passes his hands over a
few controls in preparation for the Admiral's visit.

10 EXT. STRUCTURE AND SURROUNDINGS - LATER SAME DAY   10

The researchers on ATLAS 2 have been given the photos
taken of VO and are passing them around on deck while
Carol Barr films the structure, hoping for her own
glimpse. Admiral Tullie has informed the White House
of his conversation with VO and is now receiving
secure satellite images on the carrier.

                    CAROL
                (startled)
          My God, look at the structure !

The top of the structure begins to morph. An enormous,
razor thin, clear polygonal disk, 5,000 feet in
diameter forms overhead. Everyone on the assembled
ships look skyward in dumbfounded amazement and are
all trying to talk on the radio at the same time. On
the carrier, Admiral Tullie is trying to make sense of
the din and asks Lieutenant Ericson for assistance.

                    TULLIE
          Lieutenant, see if you can get
          everyone to shut-up for two
          minutes.

                    ERICSON
          Aye sir. (transmitting) To all
          task force units, at the request
          of Admiral Tullie and to ensure
          reliable communications, would
          everybody please shut-up for two
          minutes.

                    TULLIE
                (laughing)
          Now **that's** the way to carry out an
          order people. Well done Lieutenant.

                    ERICSON
          Thank you sir.

The com traffic dies down immediately and Admiral
Tullie intercoms air operations.

> TULLIE
> Air operations, this is Admiral
> Tullie.

> AIR BOSS (V.O.)
> Air Boss aye.

> TULLIE
> I want your best chopper pilot
> standing by to take me aloft, on
> the double.

> AIR BOSS (V.O.)
> Aye sir, be advised, heavy weather
> turning towards us...3 hours.

Admiral Tullie leaves the conference room and heads
out. He meets the crew chief in the hanger, puts on
his flying gear, trots out to the waiting helicopter
and climbs into the co-pilots position. **CAPTAIN TUG
BRADLEY** on pilot duty.

> BRADLEY
> Looks like a hell of a day at sea
> admiral ! Where to ?

> TULLIE
> I want to get over top of this
> thing Tug.

> BRADLEY
> Aye sir, hang on.

The chopper lifts off smoothly amid the regular bustle
of daily air operations. We are immediately treated to
a panoramic view of this mammoth construct, nestled in
an endless sea. As the chopper climbs over the top,
another shape appears in their flight path.

> TULLIE
> (taps pilot's arm)
> Hey Tug, do you see that ?

> BRADLEY
> (pointing)
> Over there ? Looks like a landing
> pad.

A large polygonal bulls eye takes shape just ahead of
the chopper dead center, lights and all.

> BRADLEY
> I'm getting voice traffic sir and
> I don't think its operations. They
> are asking for you Admiral.

> TULLIE
> Patch me in.

> VO (V.O.)
> Hi Jack, thanks for coming. As you
> can see I've been getting the
> place spiffed up for company.

> TULLIE
> I imagine you don't entertain a
> lot.

> VO (V.O.)
> Not recently. I think its okay for
> you to land Jack, winds are pretty
> light across the deck.

> TULLIE
> Thank you Mr. VO, we'll be right
> down.

> BRADLEY
> Are you sure sir, we don't have
> any back-up with us ?

> TULLIE
> Hike up your Huggies Captain and
> land this bird.

> BRADLEY
> Aye sir. CORAL 1 to base, we are
> landing on the structure, will
> advise - out.

The copter touches down gently on the pad prepared by
VO and is immediately sealed to the deck under a
glowing polygonal bubble. Inside the chopper, Admiral
Tullie calls VO for an explanation.

> TULLIE
> Uh...Mr. VO, I'm a little unclear
> about the bubble over our heads.

> VO (V.O.)
> No worries guys, just a precaution
> so you don't blow away. Bad
> weather coming I'm afraid. There
> is a lift immediately to your
> left, come on down.

> BRADLEY
> We're not getting any com traffic
> at all now sir. Not even static.

> TULLIE
> Not much we can do about it now
> Tug. Lets go meet our host.

Tullie and Bradley proceed to the lift which is an
open glowing polygon on the deck. It seems to melt
through the deck as soon as they step on. They now
find themselves in a large, mostly empty room, save
for 2 chairs, a table set with sodas, cheese steaks
and a note from VO saying he has been detained and
would they please hang out awhile. As their eyes
adjust to the room light, they begin to notice the
large polygonal view screens that cover the walls.
Each with a different picture or purpose. Some are
task force ships, the approaching weather system, a
number of government installations around the world,
mines, and landfills. In addition there are several
large screens with meters showing levels of who knows
what.

> BRADLEY
> What do you think Admiral ?

> TULLIE
> I think we should eat.

Both men make themselves comfortable and watch with
fascination all the activity around them.

11 INT. PRESIDENT'S BEDROOM - 30 MINUTES LATER

The President is on her bed trying to catch a nap. VO
appears in the middle of the bedroom, in the center of
a polygonal doorway. VO is casually dressed in jeans
and a Polo style shirt. Kirby starts to stir and
cracks an eye.

> VO
> Hi Kirby, sorry to catch you
> relaxing.

Kirby bolts upright.

                    KIRBY
          Oh my God ! Who...what are you ?
          How did you get in here ?

                    VO
          Sorry Kirby, I forget that my
          entrance can be a little...
          startling. I am entertaining
          Admiral Tullie and his pilot at
          the moment and I wanted to extend
          an invitation to you as well.

                    KIRBY
          Your kidding right. Your actually
          just some Cirque Du Soleil loon
          that escaped from the tour..right ?

                    VO
               (smiling)
          No but that was a rib tickler.

                    KIRBY
          I already hit the alarm you know.

                    VO
          I assumed. It really won't impact
          my day.

                    KIRBY
          Pretty gutsy statement for a guy
          that's about to be tackled by ten
          Secret Service agents and at least
          two Marines.

                    VO
          Like I said Kirby, no big deal.

Now, as VO stands in the presence of the leader of the
free world, an assortment of pistols and crappy
attitudes comes tumbling through the door. Very
shortly thereafter all become aware that VO is encased
in pulsing, pale silver light and impossible to shift.

                    VO
          I know this Buster Keaton pile up
          must be pretty embarrassing guys
          but I'm sure Kirby thinks you
          earned your pay for the week. No
          harm done.

A middle aged man in a very nice three piece, who was the only person not clutching a gun in nervous anticipation, speaks up. Secret Service agent **THOMAS CLARK** moves between VO and the President.

                    THOMAS
          Are you okay chief ?

                    KIRBY
          I'm fine so far Tom.

                    THOMAS
          Who's this...guy ?

                    KIRBY
          Sorry Tom, don't know yet.

                    THOMAS
          How did he get in here ?

                    KIRBY
          Your job Tom, sorry you missed it.

Tom turns to VO.

                    THOMAS
          You're probably in a ton of
          trouble son.

                    VO
          I was sure that would be your
          immediate attitude but before we
          continue, may I use the restroom ?

                    THOMAS
          You've got stones man, I'll give
          you that.

                    KIRBY
          We've already covered that Tom and
          I was hoping to get a little rest
          this evening. Alright, everyone
          with a gun **except Tom**, please
          clear the room but stay close.

                    VO
          I hate to interrupt folks but I
          really gotta go. Its just like
          hide and seek, you settle into a
          good spot and your water bag goes
          haywire. Who knew !

                              KIRBY
Tom

                              THOMAS
Yes chief ?

                              KIRBY
                    (gesturing)
Please escort, uh...I didn't catch
your name son.

                              VO
Please, call me VO.

                              KIRBY
Escort Mr. VO to the restroom down
the hall.

                              THOMAS
Ma'am ?

                              KIRBY
Look Tom, not to be dictatorial or
anything but if your people had
found this man first, maybe he
would have peed **before** he got to
my bedroom.

                              VO
Come on Tom, buck up. It wasn't
your fault and you couldn't have
stopped me anyway.

                              THOMAS
God.

                              VO
That's the spirit. Don't go away
Kirby, I'll be right back.

                              KIRBY
You sound pretty sure of that son.

VO chuckles, smiles and steps out of his doorway,
which disappears in a blink. Tom walks VO down the
hall through a contingent of nervous and bemused faces.

                              VO
                    (politely)
Can we hurry this along Tom ?

                          THOMAS
             Does this glow go everywhere with
             you ?

                          VO
             Yup, next question.

                          THOMAS
             OK, why did you call the President
             Kirby instead of her formal title ?

                          VO
             I don't like titles Tom. Never use
             em.

                          THOMAS
             But she **is** the leader of the free
             world and so forth.

                          VO
             I know, I just met her. Eat more
             fish Tom, brain food I understand.

                          THOMAS
             Watch it smart ass, she said take
             you, she didn't say anything about
             bringing you back.

                          VO
             I'm certain that was understood
             Tom. You know, I like the way you
             handle yourself. I could tell you
             were in authority.

                          THOMAS
             May I ask how ?

                          VO
             Your suit isn't wrinkled, you
             obviously supervise on your feet.

                          THOMAS
             I need a drink.

The two arrive at their destination but can't get
through the crowd. Tom takes charge and it's like
trying to part the Red Sea.

                          THOMAS
             C'mon people, make a hole !

                        THOMAS (CONT'D)
                   Alright Mr. VO, lets not keep the
                   President waiting.

VO heads into the bathroom, nice but unremarkable
considering the surroundings and tends to business.

                        VO (THINKING)
                   Wonder what's going on outside my
                   hearing...pretty sure they'll try
                   to keep me in and hustle Kirby
                   out...(chuckles) Tom is in for a
                   shock, he doesn't know I sealed
                   off Kirby's bedroom...what time is
                   it...better quit futsing around...

VO pops up in Kirby's bedroom again and she has re-
dressed.

                        VO
                   Hi Kirby, it's me again.

                        KIRBY
                   I wish you would use the door like
                   normal people and may I ask what
                   happened to Tom ?

                        VO
                   He has probably discovered I am no
                   longer in the restroom and is
                   running furiously in this
                   direction.

                        PRESIDENT
                   You do seem to have that effect on
                   people.

                        VO
                   Don't worry Kirby, enlightenment
                   is forthcoming.

The President's doorway is covered in pale silver
light. Security personnel can be seen in the adjoining
room shouting in the President's direction but no
sound can be heard. Tom now comes into the adjoining
room.

                        VO
                   I see Tom is back. Let's have him
                   in here shall we, sort of round
                   out our group.

                                KIRBY
               OI !

                                VO
               You're pretty hard to flap Kirby,
               I like that. Stay tough, you will
               probably need that at some point.

                                KIRBY
               Tough doesn't sound particularly
               good Mr. VO. Sounds like I should
               be... apprehensive, at least.

                                VO
               That's the spirit.

VO motions towards the door, a silver filament leaps
from his fingertips to Tom and he comes floating
through the silver film covering the doorway. Everyone
is momentarily speechless.

                                VO
               You look a little pale Tom,
               feeling alright ?

                                THOMAS
               Do you travel like that all the
               time ?

                                VO
               Have a seat Tom, Kirby and I were
               about to chat.

                                THOMAS
               Chief ?

                                KIRBY
               Have a seat Tom.

                                THOMAS
               If you say so chief.

                                VO
               Let us say for the moment, that
               everything I tell you is accurate,
               truthful and trustworthy.

                                THOMAS
               So we shouldn't think you are
               completely stuffed full of wild
               blueberry muffins ?

                          KIRBY
          Good one Tom.

                          THOMAS
          Thanks chief, its from "The Thing".

                          VO
          You are the first of several
          people I wish to chat with. This
          planet has big problems and I
          think I can help in a big way.

                          THOMAS
          Wasn't this Hitler's schtick ?

Kirby snickers.

                          VO
               (smiling)
          If you will look at this.

VO points and a large polygonal screen has appeared in
the room. The images of Admiral Tullie and Captain
Bradley pop up. They have just finished lunch and are
seen observing the many monitors in the room.

                          VO
          Hi Jack...Tug, I hope lunch was
          satisfactory.

                          TULLIE
               (looking around)
          Best cheese steak I ever ate,
          thank you.

                          VO
          Jack, I am here with the President
          and Tom Clark. I have invited them
          to visit also. Can you hold on
          there for another hour or so ?

                          TULLIE
          We could use a bathroom break.
          Tug's back teeth are floating.

                          VO
          About 100 steps to starboard guys.
          Follow the blue light. Its not
          what you are used to but you'll
          figure it out.

                        TULLIE
            Madam President ?

                        KIRBY
            Go ahead Admiral.

                        TULLIE
            Ma'am, although we have been very
            well treated by our host, I'm not
            comfortable with you visiting here
            un-escorted.

                        THOMAS
            I must agree with the Admiral
            chief. I think, if you are even
            contemplating the offer, that you
            should have some kind of security
            detail. Anything less would be
            irresponsible on our part.

                        KIRBY
            Mr. VO ?

                        VO
            Sure but my home is protected by
            automatic systems, so don't bring
            anyone that can't play nice and no
            weapons. You can bring your sneaky
            spy stuff, it won't work but you
            can bring it.

                        KIRBY
            I want to bring Tom and Elaine
            Kellog, My science adviser, okay?

                        VO
            You betcha. We can all leave from
            here as soon as you're ready.

                        KIRBY
            Tom, you go and find four people
            that had good toilet training and
            get back here on the double.
            Admiral, go ahead and stay where
            you are and we'll be there within
            the hour.

                        TULLIE
            Understood. Mr. VO, can I
            communicate with my ships ?

                         VO
          Sure thing Jack. Find the screen
          with the carrier on it and just
          talk, they will hear you. Oh, you
          don't need to say over or anything.

                       KIRBY
          Admiral, don't say anything about
          me coming to anyone.

                       TULLIE
          Affirmative.

The screen disappears and VO turns to Tom.

                         VO
               (motioning)
          Go ahead Tom.

                       THOMAS
          Don't you need to give me the
          fingertips or something ?

                         VO
               (smiling)
          Nah, that's mostly for show, go
          ahead and walk through.

Tom steps over the threshold and breaks into a run.

                   VO (TO KIRBY)
               (surprised)
          I didn't figure him for a sprinter.

12 INT. OFFICE OF PROF. ODETTE HUME - SIMULTANEOUS DAY

A polygonal doorway pops up in the New York office of
professor **ODETTE HUME**, theoretical physicist and out
steps VO.

                         VO
          Hi Odette, how's your day going ?

                       ODETTE
          Uh...Hi there...I'm not
          hallucinating this am I ? I just
          had a couple energy shots.

                         VO
          No, I'm real Odette. Please, call
          me VO.

                              ODETTE
          Just VO, not like VO the really
          inexplicable or something ?

                              VO
          Nope, just VO. Odette, you're on a
          short list of scientific talent on
          the desk of the President's
          Science Adviser, Elaine Kellog.

                              ODETTE
          I hadn't heard anything, what's
          the story ?

                              VO
          I have arranged a meeting at my
          home with the President, a couple
          of her associates and some Navy
          people. I would like very much for
          you to attend.

                              ODETTE
          Where, exactly, is your home ?

                              VO
          The Marianas trench, off the coast
          of Guam. The Navy is already in
          attendance and the President will
          arrive within the hour. Can I
          count you in ?

                              ODETTE
          New York is a long way from Guam,
          even assuming you have a better
          way to get there. I assume you do,
          I mean, you did bring your own
          doorway and you are covered with
          glowing polygons and everything.

                              VO
          Correct Odette. We can be there in
          a few minutes. You want to go
          plain or fancy ?

                              ODETTE
          I have no idea what either of
          those entail but I'll definitely
          take fancy

                              VO
          Hang on.

VO steps into the doorway and points towards Professor
Hume. A silver filament leaps from his fingertips and
brings Odette in. The door disappears in a silver
flash.

13 <u>EXT. GULF OF MEXICO - SIMULTANEOUS DAY</u>   13

Marine and evolutionary biologist **JANE COLUCCI** is on a
small research boat in the Gulf of Mexico taking water
samples over the side, when a polygonal doorway
appears, right in front of her, at the stern. Jane
jumps out of her skin.

                         VO
              Hi Jane, sorry to pop in on you
              this way.

Jane grabs for her diving knife.

                         JANE
              How the hell did you get on my
              boat ? Why are you covered in
              glowing polygons ? Who the hell
              are you ?

                         VO
              Jane, please try to...

                         JANE
              Look pal, I'm not some frail
              little girl. You move and I'll
              carve you like a pumpkin.

VO has both hands in the air and backs up slightly.

                         VO
              Please calm down Jane, I'm only
              here to talk.

                         JANE
              Then talk and be damn quick about
              it.

                         VO
              My name is VO, I came to invite
              you to a meeting at my home. There
              are others already on their way.

                         VO
              So, already scared the crap out of
              other people today have you ?

Jane is slowly making her way over to the marine radio.

                    VO
          Yup. I have an interesting
          research opportunity for you.

                    JANE
          The only thing I'm going to help
          you with is a ride on a Coast
          Guard cutter.

Jane now has her hand on the radio and is trying to
get a signal out but discovers its not functional.

                    VO
          Sorry Jane, I can't let you
          involve anyone else right now.

Jane sits down and puts her head in her hands.

                    JANE
          This can't be happening, it just
          can't. I got stung or
          something ... I'm hallucinating...

                    VO
          Would you feel better if you could
          speak with someone else that's
          involved, a fellow professional ?

                    JANE
          I'd feel better if I had a bigger
          knife...but...I suppose it
          couldn't hurt.

VO gestures and an image appears in the doorway. It is
the President getting ready for the meeting.

                    VO
          Hi Kirby, glad to see you again.
          I'd like you to meet someone.

Kirby is with Tom Clark, Elaine Kellog and four large
men in suits. All do a double take at the very
confusing sight before their eyes. VO times two.

                    KIRBY
          But...You're...How ? You're
          standing right here in this room ?
          How is this possible ?

                          VO
              It's mostly math Kirby. Please say
              hi to Jane Colucci, marine
              biologist and one of Elaine's top
              ten I believe.

                          KIRBY
              Hi Jane, I'm Kirby Shirrah. Nice
              to have you aboard.

                          VO
              Actually Kirby, Jane has balked a
              bit at joining the group.

                          ELAINE KELLOG
              Hi Jane, I'm Elaine Kellog, the
              President's Science Adviser. You
              were going to be contacted by my
              office but Mr. VO beat me to it.

Jane throws her hands in the air.

                          JANE
              Alright, alright, I give up.

                          VO
                     (to the other VO)
              Fantastic ! Take good care of
              everyone VO, we'll see you soon.

Back on Jane's boat, the image has disappeared and VO
moves towards the doorway.

                          VO
              Ready Jane ?

                          JANE
              I can't just abandon the boat, I
              borrowed it.

                          VO
              You'll be back in a couple hours.

VO holds Jane's hand and walks into the doorway which
promptly blinks out.

14 <u>INT. HOME OF DOC. BENJAMIN DARIUS - SIMUL. DAY</u>   14

DOCTOR DARIUS, aeronautics and space engineer and
current head of NASA, is having a quiet meal at home.
VO appears in a polygonal doorway with a silver flash.

                              VO
          Hi Ben, what's on the menu ?

                              BEN
          Jesus Christ man !

                              VO
          I get that a lot.

                              BEN
          No kidding. You want to tell me
          why you broke into my house ?

                              VO
          Broke In is an ugly term Ben, I
          prefer...made an appearance.

                              BEN
          On a first name basis are we ?

                              VO
          Sorry Ben, I forgot my manners.
          Please, call me VO.

It is only now that Ben realizes that VO is covered
head to toe in glowing polygons and he brought his own
doorway.

                              BEN
          Good god man, what are you ? Where
          are you from ?

                              VO
          Closer than you might think Ben
          but for now, I need your help.

                              BEN
          With what ?

                              VO
          The experience of a lifetime Ben.
          Take a short trip to my home in
          the Marianas.

                              BEN
          I must be nuts but I'll come
          along. I have **got** to see what
          makes you glow. So what now ?

                              VO
          Just take my hand Ben.

Ben and VO join hands and walk through.

15 <u>INT. THE WALL - PACIFIC OCEAN - SIMULTANEOUS DAY</u> 15

Inside the room where Admiral Tullie and Captain
Bradley are cooling their heels, four doorways spring
up. Through one comes VO One with the President, Tom
Clark, Elaine Kellog and the four security men,
another with Odette Hume and VO Two, VO Three with Ben
Darius and VO four with Jane Colucci. Rapt faces
marvel at one another and the sight of four VO.

>   ALL FOUR VO TOGETHER
>   Welcome to our home everyone.

Three of the four VO walk back into their individual
doorways which then slide together with the fourth and
blink out. One VO remains.

>   VO
>   I guess introductions are in
>   order. I think everyone knows
>   President Shirrah. This is Tom
>   Clark of the Secret Service, the
>   President's Science Adviser,
>   Elaine Kellog, Professor Odette
>   Hume, Doctor Benjamin Darius of
>   NASA, Doctor Jane Colucci, Admiral
>   Jack Tullie and Captain Tug
>   Bradley, both of the U.S. Navy and
>   of course the President's security
>   detail. Questions ?

The air is instantly filled with coincident questions
and no one is actually listening for answers.

>   VO
>   Okay, question and answer time is
>   N.G.. Let's take a tour instead.

Just then, an otherworldly klaxon sounds, like
tinkling bells with a cats meow. VO moves to the large
polygonal screen that is monitoring the approaching
storm system and motions the Admiral over.

>   VO
>   Looks pretty serious JACK.

>   ADMIRAL
>   I have to move the ships away.

                              VO
          No, tell your surface ships to
          move closer, well under the disk.
          You've got about fifty minutes.

                          ADMIRAL
          What are you going to do ?

                              VO
          Go to the same screen you used
          earlier and tell them to hurry.

As Admiral Tullie makes his way to the carrier view
screen, VO passes his hands over several gauges and a
dozen T'AH come out of the walls, manipulating even
more gauges and indicators. The interior glow becomes
more and more intense. Odette breaks the silence.

                      ODETTE HUME
                (points at the T'AH)
          What the hell are those things ?

                              VO
          They are called T'AH. They are
          intelligent constructs...helpers.

                      ELAINE KELLOG
          I need more people, this is
          incredible.

                          ADMIRAL
          We're moving Mr. VO, twenty five
          minutes to get everyone in place.

                              VO
          We're ready here Jack.

The last vessel moves under the enormous disk and a
curtain of glowing polygons leaps from the entire disk
edge and forms a vertical tube. It shoots straight up
through sixty thousand feet and down to the bottom of
the trench. It is now dead calm like the eye of a
hurricane, no wind, no sound but a couple of sea birds.

                            BEN
          What just happened ?

                              VO
          Come outside everybody and have a
          look.

The assembled group takes the lift up to the deck. The
storm is raging all around outside the enormous column
but the sea below is like glass. The ships are still,
like toys in a bathtub. Kirby puts her hand on VO's
shoulder.

                    KIRBY
          You're not from around here are
          you ?

                    VO
          The storm should blow past us in
          four or five hours. Let's take
          that tour shall we. We'll skip the
          lift for this one.

A new doorway folds up from the deck and VO motions
for all to proceed through. VO is the last one in and
the door disappears in a silver flash. Now in a new,
dimly lit room. Everyone extends their hands so they
don't bump into anything.

                    JANE
          Its pretty dark in here VO.

                    VO
          Sorry folks, I forgot to leave the
          porch light on.

VO waves his hand, the outside of the walls brighten
up to reveal an alien landscape under their feet few
humans have ever seen.

                    VO
          There, that's better.

                    JANE
          What am I seeing ? Where are we ?

                    VO
          You are at the bottom of your
          worlds deepest trench, thirty
          eight thousand feet down. Want to
          do a little exploring Jane ?

                    JANE
          Hell yeah ! How ?

                    VO
          Just walk forward, the wall will
          stay ahead of you.

Jane walks tentatively towards the wall, it deforms
into a corridor that keeps pace with her every step. A
variety of deep sea denizens, attracted by the light,
swim, crawl and squiggle around and beneath her.

> JANE
> Feels like we're still at surface
> pressure ?

> ODETTE
> How does the wall withstand this
> depth, it's so thin ?

> BEN
> And why aren't we touching bottom ?

> ELAINE
> Are we floating ?

> VO
> Alright folks, one more move and
> then story time.

A new doorway opens and the congregation ambles
through, reappearing in a cavernous space with a
vaulted ceiling so high, it seems to go on forever.
The same polygons make up the entire room and floating
all around are brightly glowing T'AH that are
interfacing with hundreds of screens. Images from all
over the earth and fantastic cosmic vistas of all
descriptions shift continuously.

> ADMIRAL
> Not wishing to be ungracious Mr.
> VO but why are you watching these
> military installations ?

> VO
> Don't worry Jack, they're not all
> yours. I'm an equal opportunity
> snoop.

> KIRBY
> This is overwhelming...**wow** !

> VO
> Story time.

Recliners form up from the floor, as well as a table
and giant view screen. Everyone takes a seat and
braces for further amazement.

                         VO
          Make your selves comfortable. Is
          anyone hungry, I can order out.

                    ODETTE
          I can't wait to see where.

Spontaneous laughter infects the group.

                         VO
          I'll send myself. Arby's ?

The assembly nods in approval and VO 2 appears in a
doorway, waves and disappears.

                         VO
          Once upon a time, about 8,000
          Earth years ago, give or take a
          decade, I made a semi crash
          landing into your planet while
          sight seeing on this side of the
          galaxy.

VO pauses for a moment to let people catch their
breath. Wide eyes and slack jaws tell the tale.

                         VO
          I hit going, well, pretty fast. I
          hit so fast in fact that I ended
          up sinking to the bottom of this
          trench. You are inside what is
          actually my space ship and I am,
          as of today, 102,856 years old.
          Questions ?

                    BEN
          Holy Methuselah Batman !

                    ELAINE
          Amen brother.

                    ODETTE
          Uh, why polygons ? I mean...you
          know...why polygons ?

                         VO
          Think carbon ODETTE.

                    ODETTE
          Are you talking about Graphene ?

                         VO
          Supersized. Every polygon is 1,000
          sections thick, networked together.
          Individual polygons are linked to
          the quantum signature of a mapped
          stellar object, pulsar, nebula,
          black hole, planet, star or they
          contains fusion reactions. Some
          have both, some other functions
          such as ship command and control
          or the view screens you see around
          you, signal processing and so on.

                         ELAINE
          Some of those involve very high
          energies, radiation, magnetic
          fields. Why aren't we effected ?

                         VO
          Each section, even though they are
          physically connected, exist in
          their own quantum states. States
          which never interact with other
          states under normal circumstances
          but can be connected together to
          produce higher energy potentials
          and other combined quantum states.

                         KIRBY
          I'm lost.

                         TUG
          Me too.

                         JANE
          I'm not proud, help !

                         VO
          How about you Elaine ?

                         ELAINE
          You know what, I'm good.

                         BEN
          I think I have a handle on this.
          You're saying, for instace, that
          the ships' skin exists in the same
          quantum state as the water at any
          depth, so it's as if there is an
          equal amount of water on either
          side, all pressure equalized.

                              VO
          Correct.

                           ODETTE
          And we travel between places by
          matching the quantum state of that
          location with where we are now.

                              VO
          Correct. And each section can
          match energy states, with as many
          of the energetic sections as
          necessary, to power that activity.

                             BEN
          So we can go anywhere you've
          already mapped...any distance ?

                              VO
          Neat huh.

VO two steps out of a doorway with several large bags
of food and drink.

                            VO 2
          Chow time.

VO 2 sets down his groceries on the table, turns and
disappears into the doorway. The group continues the
discussion as they move to the table. The large screen
lights up and SHREK starts to play in the background.

                              VO
          I love this movie.

Tom notices that VO is not eating.

                            TOM
          Don't you eat Mr. VO ?

                              VO
          I don't have to but I've developed
          a serious weakness for some Earth
          stuff, like cheese steaks.

                           TULLIE
          That I understand.

                           KIRBY
          Let's get back to you Mr. VO. You
          say you crashed ?

                         VO
Yup.

                         KIRBY
I don't understand something, the
way you just walk between places,
how does a crash happen ?

                         VO
I was trying to avoid a gamma ray
burst while traveling in normal
space but I wasn't fast enough. My
emergency systems couldn't handle
it all and everything overloaded,
kind of a cosmic pothole.

                    TUG (QUOTE FINGERS)
How fast is **"not fast enough"**.

                         VO
My ship, itself, is a mono-pole
and because it has virtualy no
mass, I can travel at the speed of
light.

                         ODETTE
A mono pole, that's incredible.
Until today, mono-poles were only
theoretical...on this planet
anyway.

                         VO
I can move the entire ship through
a section but I only do that to
get to a general area. After a
large energy expediture the ship
needs to rebuild reserves and as
you know, there's nothing like
seeing the sights in a Winnebago.

                         KIRBY
Mr. VO, this has been wonderful
and we are all grateful that you
chose us to visit but I suspect it
wasn't just for dinner and a show.

                         VO
Correct, my ship was so heavily
damaged in the crash, I took a nap
and let the T'AH get on...(CONT'D)

                         VO (CONT'D)
          with repairs but when our supply
          of raw material was exhausted they
          woke me up.

                         KIRBY
          That was quite a nap. Are you
          operational now ?

                         VO
          Mostly but I knew I was going to
          need a little help so I sent out a
          signal to get your attention.

                         KIRBY
          Let me guess, the B-52s ?

                         VO
                    (smiling)
          Wonderfully odd aren't they.

                         ODETTE
          How long did it take to learn our
          language ? Your very proficient.

                         VO
          Not long. VO is surprisingly close
          to English. Similar phonetics,
          slightly different rules, similar
          sentence structure, a few extra
          letters. I mostly watched a lot of
          television.

                         KIRBY
          That explains a few things.

                         ELAINE
          I know everybody is dying to ask
          this one, where are you from ?

                         VO
          I am from the opposite side of
          this galaxy. We VO tend to not die
          ever, so I'm pretty sure they are
          still around but I have been cut
          off for so long I can't be sure.

                         BEN
          Have you tried to contact your
          people yet ?

                              VO
              The T'AH started to send an
              emergency call about ten years
              ago. Since it would only have
              taken them an hour or so to
              respond, I think they might have
              moved on. The T'AH only sent the
              signal to the home worlds last
              known location and it travels
              around. I would have to conduct a
              systematic search at this point.

                            ODETTE
              Only an hour to get a signal to
              the other side of the galaxy and
              your whole planet travels...wow.

                              VO
              Yeah, give or take a minute. Its
              going to be a bit tougher to find
              them now. Oh well, poop happens.

                            KIRBY
              You **do** watch a lot of television.

                            TULLIE
              Sorry to interrupt Mr. VO but it
              looks like the storm is breaking
              up. We should be heading back.

                            JANE
              Speak for yourself Admiral. I
              would **love** to walk around the
              bottom again !

                            KIRBY
              No, we probably should go before
              people get worried about us.

                              VO
              Kirby, I transmitted your entire
              visit to Jack's ship and the White
              House but you're right. I'll get
              you all started.

VO gestures to the T'AH and doorways appear that lead
to the White House, Ben Darius's home, Odette's
office, Jane's boat and the helicopter on deck. The
outside wall surrounding the ships is absorbed back
into the disk as is the bubble over the chopper.

                          VO
              I'm glad you all enjoyed your
              visit folks but I have quite a bit
              more to accomplish today anyhow.

                          ELAINE
              So this is it ?

                          ODETTE
              Can we come back ? I've got a
              thousand more questions and Ben
              looks like he's gonna cry.

                          BEN
              I feel like momma is dragging me
              out of the candy store...

                          VO
              Don't worry, I have no immediate
              plans to leave. Also, you'll want
              to keep an eye on this structure,
              its going to change again soon.

Everyone shakes hands and moves to their respective
doorways. All step through and arrive instantly at
their destinations. Admiral Tullie and Captain Bradley
climb aboard the chopper and take off. Alone now, VO
stands in the ships great room surrounded, as always,
by floating T'AH. The pace of activity in the ship,
the wall and the disk triples. VO collapses into his
big recliner and closes his eyes.

16 <u>INT. TELEVISION SCREENS WORLDWIDE - DAYTIME</u>   16

Satellites from every country are now watching the
enormous structure in the Pacific. Ships of all sizes
and descriptions have converged on Guam to witness,
first hand, this incredible sight. Naval intelligence
was right, the cordon could not be enforced now that
the word was out. The President has moved the task
force out to a respectful distance and is engaged in
traffic control only. Then, without warning, the
entire assembly suddenly folds into itself and
disappears beneath the waves. The civilian ships
linger for a day or so then slowly depart. The Navy
has informed the President and the task force is
ordered to pull back after 3 days when no further
contact is made with VO. The U.S. Subs, however,
remain submerged close by to maintain surveillance.

President Shirrah is reporting to Congress on their
visit with Mr. VO.

                        CNN
Word from anonymous government sources has reached CNN
that a group of U.S. citizens may have actually been
inside a mysterious structure in the Pacific and this
press conference by the President may shed light on
that specific event. In attendance are news teams from
every country, large and small. We understand that the
hall has been specially prepared with large video
monitors just for this broadcast but no word on what
we will be seeing.

                    BBC AMERICA
Under strict security, even reporters from unfriendly
nations have been allowed to attend this press
conference. The BBC has been told by a confidential
source that President Shirrah may, in fact, be
detailing her **own experience** with the object. Some
excitement to the left now and it appears the
President is about to enter the hall. (all rise)

President Shirrah strides confidently to the podium.

                        KIRBY
             My fellow Americans and all the
             citizens of the world. I want to
             share with you the extraordinary
             events of the last few days and
             the amazing experience I and a
             small group of scientists and U.S.
             Naval personnel have shared. As
             you all are now aware from the
             news services, a large structure
             appeared out of the undersea
             trench off the coast of Guam, near
             the area known as Challenger Deep.

Kirby motions to the large monitors. Film of the
structure, the disk as it formed, the R.O.V. footage
at the bottom of the trench, the film of VO waving and
a host of photos.

                    KIRBY (CONT'D)
             We first learned of this object
             from Doctor Carol Barr of the
             research vessel Atlas 2. It was
             their robotic vehicle that found
             the structure at the bottom of the
             trench before it broke the surface.

                              KIRBY (CONT'D)
Some of these details are in your
handouts but I want to tell you
first hand what we discovered.

An extraterrestrial being who
calls himself VO made himself
known to us. He is somewhat
different in appearance to us as
you can see from these photographs
and told us he is over 180,000
years old. His ship crashed on
Earth some 8,000 years ago and he
became trapped at the bottom of
the Marianas trench. The structure
and Vo's ship are one and the same.

The only reason the United States
was first on the scene, according
to VO, was that he saw the
submersible from Atlas 2 and
decided to **"Say Hi"**.

Doctor Barr contacted Woods Hole
Oceanographic and they, in turn,
notified the Navy and White House.

VO first made contact with Admiral
Tullie of Naval Task Group 3 which
was already on duty in the area at
the time. VO also appeared to
myself, Secretary of Defense Bob
Maxwell, my Science Adviser Elaine
Kellog, astrophysicist Odette
Hume, NASA Director Benjamin
Darius and evolutionary biologist
Jane Colucci.

We were all taken, by means we do
not yet fully understand, into his
ship and were all treated to a
meal, a movie and this story.

VO also told us he has been
hibernating until very recently
and has been attempting to contact
his race without success. I feel
certain that VO will communicate
again and give us an opportunity
to know him better.

                           KIRBY (CONT'D)
                    VO may choose to contact others
                    and although we would encourage
                    you to let someone know, our group
                    never felt threatened in any way
                    and were treated with great
                    respect. Well, that's all the
                    information we have for now.

                    Thank you all for your kind
                    attention and I am certain there
                    is more excitement to come.

The President leaves congress to thunderous applause.
All of the news media go wild with endless speculation
as well as all the serious science and paranoid
crappola that are the opposing hallmarks of humanity.

18 INT. OVAL OFFICE - WHITE HOUSE - LATER SAME DAY   18

The President is heading back to the Oval Office for a
private briefing with the U.S. intelligence community,
to discuss dealing with a possible panic and or
unfriendly states bent on doing something stupid.
Elaine Kellog is already in the room as Kirby enters.
VO is coming.

                           ELAINE
                    Why am I sitting in Kirby, this
                    intelligence stuff isn't really my
                    speed.

                           KIRBY
                    I know Elaine but I need someone
                    here from academia in case they
                    ask a sciency question.

Just then a polygonal doorway pops up in the office
and VO steps through.

                           VO
                    Hi ladies, may I come in ?

                           KIRBY
                       (smiling)
                    You're a little **in** to be asking.

                           VO
                       (face in hands)
                    Oh no, not another senseless
                    interpersonal faux pas.

Kirby and Elaine break up.

                    ELAINE
          What's that from ?

                    VO
          BBC Open University.

                    KIRBY
          Good to see you again Mr. VO. What
          may we do for you ?

                    VO
          I need your help.

                    KIRBY
          With what pray tell ?

                    VO
          You're having an anti-panic
          meeting right ?

                    KIRBY
          Uh...yeah.

                    VO
          I'm working on my ship and I need
          some more raw materials.

                    KIRBY
          And this is where the panic part
          comes in ?

                    VO
          Some of what I need might make
          some people nervous. I want you to
          assure them that it is unwarranted.

                    ELAINE
          Like what ?

                    KIRBY
          Yeah, like what ?

                    VO
          Like all the nuclear waste the
          U.S. just buried in that salt mine
          in Utah. I need it for conversion.

                    KIRBY
          Conversion into what ?...(CONT'D)

                    KIRBY (CONT'D)
Its useless, extremely dangerous
garbage. I mean, that's why we
buried it in the first place.

                    VO
Garbage to you, very helpful to
me. My ship can convert anything
into anything but the higher the
particle energy, the better for my
process. The great news is that it
won't be an environmental threat
any more. Pretty neat huh.

                    ELAINE
The NRC will go ape, they'll never
allow it. It took us ten years
just to get permission to stick it
in there.

                    KIRBY
Elaine is right Mr. VO. I couldn't
allow that without a thorough
review of your process and
something to prove, to our
satisfaction, that it will not
pose a safety hazard if moved and
reprocessed by you.

                    VO
Oh dear.

                    KIRBY
What ? You already did it didn't
you.

                    VO
There is a doorway open over the
site as we speak. Sorry Kirby, I
didn't think you'd object. Its so
much better for everyone.

                    KIRBY
I'll have to ask you to stop VO.

                    VO
Oh dear.

                    KIRBY
What ? Oh crap, its already gone
isn't it ?

                    VO
Yup.

                  ELAINE
Any other surprises today Mr. VO ?

                    VO
Actually, its a pretty long list.
If you didn't like that one you're
probably going to be really
unhappy about the rest.

                  KIRBY
Okay, lets have it. **All** of it.

                    VO
Gold, silver, platinum, methane,
uranium, hydrogen, deuterium,
copper, silicon, plutonium and a
bunch of other elements you'll
never miss. Most of this stuff
exists in sufficient quantities on
the bottom of the oceans but I had
to go further afield for the rest.

                  KIRBY
From where, I'm afraid to ask.

                    VO
I don't think anyone will say
anything in public because they
will want to avoid the whole panic
thing but pretty much everywhere.

                  KIRBY
Like ?

                    VO
Like, for instance, Fort Knox
echoes more than it used to and
your nuclear missiles aren't
nuclear so much anymore. Don't
worry though, I picked on
everybody not just you guys.

                  KIRBY
             (vert upset)
Our defense as a nation depends
largely on our nuclear forces. If
word gets out, the United States
could be wide open to attack.

                        VO
        Easy Kirby, I told you, I picked
        on everybody. No one has any
        weapons grade nuclear material at
        all. I also took all of the
        reactor grade material from all
        except your democratic nations.
        I'll take all that later, you
        won't need it.

                        ELAINE
        So, for example, North Korea and
        Iran have no nuclear material ?

                        VO
        None.

                        KIRBY
        You've been a busy boy.

                        VO
        What you will get in return will
        more than make up for it Kirby.

                        KIRBY
        What are we getting in return ?

                        VO
                (smiling)
        If I tell you now, you won't be
        surprised at Christmas.

                        KIRBY
                (rolls her eyes)
        I don't think I can handle many
        more surprises today.

                        VO
        That's the spirit.

VO walks back through the doorway and vanishes in a
silver blink. Elaine and Kirby are alone.

                        ELAINE
        The whole world is going to think
        we're responsible for this mess.

                        KIRBY
        Even the E.U. is going to think
        this is some sort of U.S. power
        grab. I better get on the phone.

                          ELAINE
        Do you want me to tell the
        scientists anything or wait ?

                          KIRBY
        Nothing they can do about any of
        this. No, not right now.

                          ELAINE
        Should I still stay for the
        meeting ?

                          KIRBY
        No, I want you to get on the phone
        with Utah and get me a first hand
        report. Make sure there is no
        residual radiation leaking out.

                          ELAINE
        I'm on it chief.

Elaine leaves. Kirby bangs her head on the desk and
buzzes her secretary **COLLETTE SMYTHE**.

                          KIRBY
        Collette ?

                          COLLETTE (V.O.)
        Yes chief ?

                          KIRBY
        I need a doughnut, quick.

                          COLLETTE
        Coming up chief...oh, everyone is
        here for the meeting. Do you want
        me to send them in yet ?

                          KIRBY
        Yeah, go ahead but don't forget my
        doughnut.

The representatives of the intelligence agencies and
Colonel Batii file in.. Collette brings in coffee for
the group and a doughnut for Kirby. The meeting opens.

                          KIRBY
        One, Elaine Kellog is handling all
        the VO science stuff for now. Two,
        Mr. VO was just here and you're
        not going to believe this one.

19 <u>EXT. MARIANAS VO STRUCTURE - DAWN - NEXT MORNING</u> 19

A new structure suddenly shoots out of the water. It
is a polygon 10 miles across that dashes up to one
mile above sea level and stops. A polygonal dish
unfurls around the upper edge of the column and a deep
depression forms in the center. The dish grows to one
hundred miles across and five miles deep. An
incredible sight by itself, the polygons making up
this behemoth begin to hum and glow more brightly as
the immense ring starts absorbing radiant energy and
pumping it down into VO's ship. Satellite images
almost immediately appear on TV reports and government
communications systems are overwhelmed with inquiries.

20 <u>INT. VO SHIP - SIMULTANEOUS DAY</u>   20

VO is sitting in his big recliner, humming, swiveling
around and watching the hundreds of screens in the
ships great room. Now dozens of T'AH float through the
hall tending to dials and gauges registering what now
has to be gargantuan amounts of energy. The color of
the ship is changing from all pale silver to a mixture
of swirling silver and gold. The ship is using the
energy to feverishly process the few items borrowed
from the worlds governments. VO stands up and flanked
by two floating T'AH, faces the largest central
monitor. VO prepares to send out his first message for
humanity, to every video screen, everywhere.

                         VO
          Hi Earth folks, as you may have
          already heard, my name is VO and
          I'm from out of town. I'd say take
          me to your leader but that's
          fifties sci-fi and I've already
          met the President. Anyhow, Kirby
          and I had a meeting yesterday and
          I explained a little bit of what
          was happening **me** wise. In order to
          make necessary repairs to my ship,
          I had to liberate a few things
          from your respective governments.
          First, I took all the nuclear fuel
          from every weapon on your planet.
          That means no one has any atomic
          bombs, at all, anymore. Then I
          took all of the stored nuclear
          waste and reprocessed it. None of
          these things pose any danger to
          your world now. I was thinking
          about returning to my home but
          they don't seem to be...(CONT'D)

                         VO (CONT'D)
          in the same place I left them, so
          I have decided to stay and give
          you a hand with some of your more
          pesky problems. That said, I am
          going to give you a few tools to
          help you along but what ultimately
          happens is entirely up to you.
          Well, that's all for now except to
          say, (southern accent) watch the
          skies y'all cause phase two is a
          comin. Bye bye, buy bonds.

21 INT. VARIOUS FORUMS - DAYTIME - 5 DAYS LATER   21

                     PRINT NARRATION
Public discussion has reached fever pitch after VO's
broadcast. Every radio station, TV channel, internet
blog, company meeting, Twitter and email want to know
one thing. What is phase 2 ? Questions come fast but
no answers. Some people are frightened, some are
skeptical, some see conspiracy but most are hopeful of
positive change. Some of those in authority react
negatively to any hint that they could lose control.

                      DESCRIPTION
The massive dish in the Pacific now folds back into
the column which, itself, begins to grow higher. Now
twisting thinner and thinner until its barely ten feet
in diameter. The column climbs to an altitude of
twenty two thousand two hundred thirty nine miles. An
umbrella spreads out from the center, wider and wider
until it surrounds the entire planet. This gigantic
sphere, made of the same polygons that cover VO and
his ship, becomes geostationary. The world watches in
wonder as this latest event unfolds. A frantic
scramble to re-task satellites gets under way to get a
closer look at this new construct. VO goes on the air.

                         VO
          That was phase two folks, Phase
          three will commence in exactly 30
          hours. Wait, hang on, I'm getting
          a call.

Everyone hears VO answer the call which is coming in
over several screens in the ship. Its **BILL DUGGIN**, the
Director General of the BBC, hoping for an interview.

                     BILL (ON SCREEN)
          Am I addressing Mr. VO ?

                          VO
          Yup. And whom are you sir ?

                          BILL (ON SCREEN)
          Bill Duggin of the BBC sir. May I
          speak with you about doing an
          interview with us ?

                          VO
          I'm kinda in the middle of
          something Bill.

                          BILL (ON SCREEN)
          My apologies sir but I think it
          would be interesting for you and I
          to talk where people could ask you
          direct questions. Allay their
          fears, as it were, about your
          intentions. What do you think ?

                          VO
          You know what Bill, that's a
          fabulous idea. We have to do it
          soon though, where are you ?

                          BILL (ON SCREEN)
          BBC Television Center London. May
          we expect you ?

                          VO
          Sure Bill. You should bring in,
          what, fifty or so assorted human
          beings for Q & A. Seems manageable.

                          BILL (ON SCREEN)
          Done. Shall we say seven tonight ?

                          VO
          I'll be there with bells on. Do
          you suppose there is a good cheese
          steak to be had in London.

                          BILL (ON SCREEN)
          International cuisine it is. I
          look forward to meeting you sir.
          (clicks off)

                          VO
          Mmmmm, what shall I wear ?

                        PRINT NARRATION
The worlds most famous broadcast center is madly
buzzing over the first ever intergalactic interview.
Bill Duggin himself has gone into the streets of
London with his staff to gather fifty ordinary
citizens for the studio audience. A referential cross
section of races, occupations, backgrounds and faiths.
The rest of the group is fleshed out with all of the
academics that could be reached in time for the show.
A polygonal doorway pops up in front of the BBC. VO
steps out and is instantly mobbed.

                    BBC STAFFER
               Mr. Duggin come quick. Mr. VO is
               here and he is trapped in the
               crowd.

Out side Bill is trying to get to VO while BBC
technicians struggle to hook up outdoor monitors for
those unable to get in for the broadcast. VO is
waving, shaking hands and signing autographs. Bill
finally makes it over to him.

                    VO
               Hi BILL.

                    BILL
               I'm glad you made it Mr. VO. Shall
               we go in ?(puts arm around VO)

The two jostle their way in a abortive attempt to pass
unchallenged but pressing humans clamor for attention,
questions shouted in the hundreds. VO takes charge.

                    VO
               Folks, may I have your attention
               for a moment.

The cacophony momentarily subsides.

                    VO (CONT'D)
               What if Mr. Duggin arranged for
               someone to take a few questions
               from this group.

A spontaneous whoop of approval rises from the
assembly and VO whispers to Bill.

                    VO (CONT'D)
               You can do that right ?

                        BILL
              Consider it done.

The crowd parts smoothly and the two men hustle in.
Mr. Duggin shouts instructions to the staff as they go.

                        BILL
              We need a remote unit out front on
              the double and get it tied in to
              my studio. We're going to take
              questions from the crowd during
              the show.

                        VO
              You run a taut ship Bill.

                        BILL
              They are the best in the business.

                        VO
              How long until we go on ?

                        BILL
              Five or ten minutes. They have to
              get the remote set up but we can
              go ahead and get started.

                        VO
              Lead on Bill.

Pandemonium erupts as VO and Bill enter the studio.
They get seated and mic'd. The producer counts down.

                        PRODUCER
              And three..two..one..cue

                        BILL
              Good evening ladies and gentlemen,
              I'm William Duggin with our very
              special guest Mr. VO.

Sustained, enthusiastic applause

                        VO
              I'm happy to be here Bill.

                        BILL
              Before we take audience questions,
              I believe Mr. VO has a brief
              statement he'd like to make..Mr. VO

                    VO
          Hi folks, as I mentioned earlier
          I've decided to stay for awhile
          and give you a hand. For the next
          thirty hours the shell which has
          formed around your planet is going
          to scan each human and record your
          individual quantum signatures.
          Don't worry, you won't feel a
          thing. After the scan completes
          you are all going to get an early
          Christmas gift. I know, pretty
          cool right but they won't be
          wrapped because on my planet, its
          the gift that counts. These teeny,
          tiny little glowing gifts will
          descend from the shell itself,
          that's right, from space. How neat
          is that. It won't matter where you
          are and you don't have to be
          outdoors, It'll find you and
          attach itself to your forehead.
          Now I know some of you are saying
          VO, I just don't think I'll look
          good with a glowing polygon on my
          forehead but I promise you, they
          are very tasteful. A side note for
          Hindus, it **may** displace your dot.
          Bill...

                    BILL
          Wow, that's certainly a lot to
          think about. Before we throw the
          mic open, may I ask a question or
          two ?

                    VO
          Shoot.

                    BILL
          What are these gifts designed to
          do ?

                    VO
          Basically, they are designed to
          align your ideal physical-genetic
          states with your quantum state.
          Make your bodies more efficient.
          Each person will, first of all,
          feel really, really exceptional.

                    BILL
What specific benefits can we
expect other than feeling great ?

                    VO
As it re-balances your body to
take maximum advantage of your
resources, each person will very
quickly reach their ideal weight.

                    BILL
Which means ?

                    VO
Everybody will probably spend more
time on the toilet.

                    BILL
What else ?

                    VO
It will immediately correct any
physical abnormalities by re-
setting your body to its ideal
genetic condition. You'll have to
keep a close eye on what you call,
at risk individuals, because they
won't know how to deal with their
new conditions or lack thereof.

                    BILL
Example ?

                    VO
Let's say someone was confined to
a wheel chair from birth. Their
legs will begin to function but
they won't actually know **how** to
walk. They will have to be taught.

                    BILL
I understand.

                    VO
The biggest benefit is that you
will all be able to derive
nourishment from the energies
around you. Solar, gamma rays, x-
rays, cosmic rays, pretty much
anything in the electromagnetic
spectrum. You will still...(CONT'D)

                         VO (CONT'D)
          be able to eat too but in a pinch
          you can do without. Oh, I would
          still breast feed as a baby back
          up, vitamins are important.

                         BILL
          I don't know what to say. This is
          all so incredible.

                         VO
          This next part is extremely
          important Bill. The gift will not
          allow anyone to commit an act of
          violence, at all, ever again.
          There are unpleasant consequences
          associated with ignoring this fact.

                         BILL
          Seems like good news to me Mr. VO.
          Okay, lets go outside next and
          field some questions.

A staffer moves out into the crowd outside the studio
and selects a raised hand.

                         STAFFER
          Yes ma'am, you have a question ?

                         YOUNG WOMAN
          Mr. VO, do we have any say in the
          matter or are we being forced ?

                         VO
          Well ma'am, if someone brings you
          a gift for your birthday, what do
          you do with it ?

                         YOUNG WOMAN
          If I like it I keep it but If I
          don't I take it back to the store.

                         VO
          This gift is returnable also. If
          you don't want it, you can remove
          it within 48 hours but if you
          remove it, it cannot be reproduced.

                         STAFFER
          Yes sir, you have a question for
          Mr. VO ?

                    OLDER GENTLEMAN
          I have an assortment of health
          issues sir, cancer, diabetes,
          arthritis. How will I be effected ?

                    VO
          You won't have those problems
          anymore. No one will, if they
          retain the gift. If the gift is
          removed, some or all of that
          persons miseries may reappear.

                    STAFFER
               (a small boy)
          Yes young man, you have a question
          for Mr. VO ?

                    BOY
          Mr. VO, are you God ?

                    VO
          No young man I am not and I've
          never met one.

                    BOY
          My mom thinks you are.

                    VO
          Please tell your mother I said
          thank you.

The camera turns back to the studio

                    BILL
          Before we take questions in the
          studio Mr. VO, perhaps you could
          tell us about yourself.

                    VO
          What would you like to know Bill ?

                    BILL
          What is the name of your planet ?

                    VO
          VO, It's a plural term.

                    BILL
          Are you married ?

                          VO
          My race doesn't really do the
          marriage thing but I do have two
          children.

                          BILL
          Do you reproduce the same way
          humans do ?

                          VO
          Yeah, pretty much. the genetic
          scans I'm doing show that we are
          actually very similar genetically.
          I think that's pretty nifty.

                          BILL
          Nifty indeed sir. What is your
          planet like ? Any similarities to
          earth ?

                          VO
          Lots of water, lots of plants and
          animals, good average temperature,
          no real cold spots.

                          BILL
          No cold spots at all ?

                          VO
          Three suns, dead flat.

                          BILL
          Have your people ever visited
          earth before ?

                          VO
          Not that I know of but I have been
          asleep for quite awhile and we do
          travel a lot.

                          BILL
          Has your race encountered any
          other intelligent species in its
          travels ?

                          VO
          A bunch. They are all pretty nice,
          I think you'd get along.

                          BILL
          Would you care to elaborate ?

                         VO
          Long stories Bill. I will tell you
          that aliens and stuff aren't quite
          like what you see in the movies.

                         BILL
          Alright, new subject. I'm certain
          people are wondering what happens
          with these wonderful gifts if you
          decide to go home. Does the
          technology go with you or is all
          this permanent ?

                         VO
          Fair question Bill. I would leave
          enough behind to keep everything
          running and train you to operate
          and maintain all the systems.

                         BILL
          Now lets take a couple questions
          from the audience.

                         STUDIO STAFFER
          The gentleman in the gray suit.

                         MIDDLE AGED GENTLEMAN
          Mr. VO, I am a professor of
          sociology at London University. Do
          you think its wise for the human
          race to undergo such comprehensive
          change in such a short time ?

                         VO
          Sure.

                         MIDDLE AGED GENTLEMAN
          You say that with great assurance.

                         VO
          Change is inevitable sir, wherever
          it comes from but as I said
          before, I can only give you some
          tools, most of what ultimately
          changes is up to humanity, not me.

                         STUDIO STAFFER
          Yes ma'am, you have a question ?

                         OLDER WOMAN (POINTING)
          Sir, my daughter here is...(CONT'D)

                          OLDER WOMAN (CONT'D)
              pregnant and her child will not be
              born in the next 30 hours. Can
              these children receive a gift
              later ?

                          VO
              Actually ma'am, I brought one with
              me for demonstration purposes. If
              your daughter wants to come up she
              can have the very first one.

A brief discussion ensues between mother and daughter
but in the end, the young mother decides to come up.
Her child has been diagnosed with Down Syndrome.

                          YOUNG MOTHER
              Sir, I have been told that my
              child is ill, can you help ?

VO reaches into his pocket and brings out a small gold
container. He picks out a very tiny glowing polygon
and motions for her to sit down beside him.

                          VO
              Ready ?

                          YOUNG MOTHER
                    (Deep Breath)
              Ready.

VO touches the object to her forehead and holds it. He
then holds his other hand to a polygon on his cheek.
VO begins to glow brightly, a brief flash and..

                          VO
              Well, how do you feel ?

                          YOUNG MOTHER
              Wonderful, absolutely wonderful
              but what about the baby ?

                          VO
              Your little girl is fine now.

                          YOUNG MOTHER
              I'm having a girl ?

                          VO
              Yup. Remember, do not take this
              off and your daughter...(CONT'D)

                              VO (CONT'D)
              will be born with her own. And
              don't forget to breast feed.

                              YOUNG WOMAN
                        (crying, happy)
              I don't know what to say. I don't
              know how to thank you. (hugs VO)

                              VO
                        (smiling at Bill)
              This is fun stuff.

The young mother returns to her seat, the proud owner
of the very first gift and hugs her mom to death. The
audience goes wild with applause and a standing ovation

                              BILL
              I must say Mr. VO, you certainly
              know how to entertain.

                              VO
              I wish I could stay longer Bill
              but I need to get home.

                              BILL
              Mr. VO, it has been such a
              pleasure to have you here with us
              today. I hope we will have other
              opportunities to know you better
              in the near future. Also...

A staffer comes out of the wings with a brown bag.

                              BILL (CONT'D)
              We have obtained not one but two
              of the finest cheese steaks in
              London, just for you.

                              VO
                        (laughing)
              Shazam ! !

VO walks from of the studio and out to the doorway he
arrived in, applause follows him all the way. VO
waves, steps through and disappears. The BBC is on the
air with a follow up to the show.

                              BBC COMMENTATOR
              What can be said after an event
              like that folks....(CONT'D)

> Wonderful on its face but is there
> a hidden cost ? Does it even
> matter to weary populations who
> want for a better life. Is hope
> impossible to ignore and is
> something, anything, better than
> nothing ? Only time will tell.

Fourteen new twisting columns shoot up from the sea
floor spaced at regular intervals. Eight around the
equator and 6 more through longitudinal lines, north
and south replacing the original column out of
Challenger Deep which retracts back into the trench.

All connect with the orbiting shell, start collecting
radiation from space and pumping it down into VO's
ship where it will be used to produce, distribute and
power the gifts in less than ten hours. Horizontal
intersections form now between vertical connectors at
seventy eight miles above sea level. A spectacular
light show that dwarfs the Aurora Borealis captivates
the populace, as the clock ticks down.

                    PRINT NARRATION
Most governments are on high alert for stupid stunts
by less savory nations. The maniacs of the world
probably don't remember that part of phase three will
completely remove their ability to even attempt mean.
VO is back in the ship making final preparations.

<u>24 INT. PRESIDENT'S BEDROOM - SIMULTANEOUS - 2 AM   24</u>

The President is in bed watching a replay of the BBC
interview when she gets a video call on her cell phone.

                    KIRBY
          Hello ?

                    VO (ON SCREEN)
          Hey Kirby, how was your day ?

                    KIRBY
          Pretty good. I'm watching your BBC
          interview, man was CNN pissed that
          they missed that one.

                    VO
          Bill did ask me first.

                    KIRBY
          Almost time for the big event huh.

                    VO
Yup.

                    KIRBY
So, what can I do for you Mr. VO ?

                    VO
I'm going to give you some
information. Whom you entrust with
the news is entirely up to you.

                    KIRBY
Alright, let's have it.

                    VO
Two hours before the gifts are
delivered, a wave will sweep Earth
and render all your ammunition
inert, conventional weapons won't
fire. I suggest you consider
getting your military people home.

                    KIRBY
Holy crap VO. The chaos will be
unbelievable. Can't we ease into
that one ?

                    VO
Remember Kirby, after the gift is
delivered, it will not allow
anyone to commit a nasty act of
any kind. Good guy, bad guy, it
won't make any difference. The
consequences will be the same.

                    KIRBY
What consequences ? What ?

                    VO
The person who attempts nasty will
be instantly recycled into the
energy net and their quantum
signature deleted from the network.

                    KIRBY
You mean **dead** ?

                    VO
They will change states, becoming
more useful to the greater system.
If you prefer a more...(CONT'D)

Hollywood type description, I
think **erased** pretty well covers it.

                    KIRBY
I'm not sure it's progress Mr. VO.

                    VO
You're still left with the same
decision. To be stupid or not to
be stupid. This only makes you
stop and think first. Its just a
tool Kirby.

                    KIRBY
I've got a headache.

                    VO
That's the spirit. Better get
moving Kirby, we both have a full
plate today. (clicks off)

                    KIRBY
Crap !

Kirby hurries to get dressed and get back to the Oval
Office. Many frantic NATO calls to make.

25 INT./EXT. VO SHIP - EARTH - 130 MINUTES TO ZERO 25

VO and the T'AH are in the ships great room preparing
to send out the energy wave that will disable all
conventional weapons. The walls pulse with power. The
14 vertical connectors and the orbiting shell are
alive with swirling, lustrous gold and silver light.
VO begins to count down, his right hand over one of
the control screens.

                    VO
        Three..two..one..**now** !

A gargantuan torrent of energy races between the ship
and the space frame, outshining the sun and turning
night into day. The wave builds and builds until it
lets go in one massive discharge straight down. The
pulse moves along and between the vertical columns
settling over everything with a bright, filmy aura.
Then, as suddenly as it came, consolidates itself back
into the links and back into the VO ship. Only the
President and her allies know what has happened. VO
broadcasts **WAR,** by Edwin Stark, to every speaker on
the planet.

26 <u>INT./EXT. VAR. WORLD LOCATIONS - SAME DAY 11 AM</u> 26

Still reeling from the energy wave and unsure of its
meaning we see a montage of humans looking skyward in
hopeful anticipation. Some pray, most are resigned but
a palpable unease underscores the run up to the gift.

Now, the immense polygons of the orbiting net begin to
emit a multitude of brilliant, sparkling colors then
tiny glowing polygons, the gifts, start their long
deliberate descent to every man, woman and child, all
6 billion, 883 million, 33 thousand, 6 hundred and
twenty one of them. Glistening, gossamer tendrils
trail behind each gift like colored spider silk.

Over the course of an hour surface observers surveill
the atmosphere awaiting these heavenly arrivals. Mere
seconds away now, the world holds its breath. The
gifts approach and attach. Small bolts of energy run
up through the threads to the shell to record the
quantum signatures receipt then disappear. Then calm,
all misgivings forgotten as humanity basks in this
incredible feeling of well being.

A montage of humans thinking out loud as they hark
back to the interview. Am I really cosmic powered ?
Can I finish the leftovers ? Do I have extra toilet
paper in the house ? I must check with my family and
friends, can Jerry see, can mom walk ? And what of
Michael J. Fox ?

27 <u>INT. WHITE HOUSE SITUATION ROOM - NEXT DAY - 8AM</u> 27

President Shirrah is receiving reports from various
government agencies about the state of the armed
forces and civilian authorities, not all of whom have
gotten the word about the deactivation of standard
weapons. Everyone is sporting their shiny new polygons.

                    PRESIDENT
          Well...I assume everybody feels as
          good as I do.

                    LIZA NEWBORN (NSA)
          I haven't felt this good since I
          threw my husband out. I've already
          lost 5 pounds too, I **love** this
          thing.

Its only five minutes into the meeting and people are
already excusing themselves to go to the bathroom. The
meeting is in complete disarray at this point.

                         KIRBY
          I suppose this is going to go on
          all day. Oh crap, now I gotta go.

Kirby runs out of the room well ahead of her surprised
security contingent. This story is repeating itself
across the world from palaces to jungle huts. Closer
to home, the D.C. Sanitary District is having trouble
keeping up with water demand. Bob Maxwell tries to
keep the meeting going.

                         BOB
          Who has the domestic reports ?
          Mary ?

                         MARY OSTERWALD (HOMELAND SEC)
          I've got it Bob. We are still
          trying to get word out about
          weapons to the police and National
          Guard units. I have only one
          incident report so far.

                         KIRBY (WALKS BACK IN)
          What happened ?

                         MARY
          Everything come out OK chief ?

                         KIRBY
          Tee hee Mary, no raise this year.

                         MARY
          Ouch. It seems a SWAT team had
          surrounded a guy who had taken
          hostages. He stepped out of the
          building with a pistol and pulled
          the trigger. SWAT responded but
          their weapons misfired. The nut's
          gun didn't fire either but he was
          immediately swallowed up into his
          forehead...the polygon from the
          nut just vanished in a blink of
          light. Nothing left, no nut, no
          nothing, all on video.

                         KIRBY
          Holy mackerel ! VO wasn't kidding.
          We have to tell all the good guys
          not to initiate anything violent
          against anyone. Looks like self
          defense might be exempt...(CONT'D)

                              KIRBY (CONT'D)
               but I don't want to take any
               chances.

Unknown to this group, thousands of violent incidents
are causing people to wink into non existence across
the breadth of humankind. The herd is thinning, one
dumbass at a time.

                              KIRBY
               You know group, if we can control
               ourselves this could be a very
               good thing.

                              BELL CARROLL (SEC OF STATE)
               I would think outfits like Amnesty
               International will have a hissy
               fit but like Mr. VO said, everyone
               still has the choice. It seems
               fair to me.

                              BOB
               Just thinking out loud chief but
               what do we do with our armed
               forces ? We've got a hundred
               thousand uniforms in the field
               whose sole purpose is to protect
               us and our friends from stupid
               people but stupid people have
               become self destructing. Do we
               bring the whole kit and caboodle
               home ?

                              KIRBY
               That's not a bad idea Bob. Maybe
               we should, I mean, they're not
               gonna have a whole lot to do
               anymore are they ?

                              MARY
               I agree with Bob, bring them home
               right away. We may need them to
               keep order here. No one knows how
               this thing is going to play out
               with the general public yet and
               lets face it, charity begins at
               home.

                              LIZA
               Its probably a good idea to keep
               our field intelligence...(CONT'D)

                         LIZA (CONT'D)
              units working for awhile. We will
              need to know what the rest of the
              world is up to.

                         KIRBY
              I don't know. Mr. VO has given
              humanity a chance to pull it's
              head out of its collective
              backside. We can't risk
              squandering the opportunity. I'm
              leaning towards calling a world
              meeting at the U.N., invite even
              the real sucky nations. No one
              will be able to hurt or otherwise
              intimidate their populations
              anyway. If they do, they go away
              for good right ? What could be
              better, everybody has to play nice
              whether they like it or not.

                         ELAINE
              Maybe a world scientific advisory
              council to handle repercussions of
              the VO technology.

                         BELL
              We might be able to sell that,
              although some of the dumber
              leaders might balk, I think its
              worth a shot chief.

                         KIRBY
              Alright, let's get something put
              together I can present to the U.N.

                         LAYNIE VAL (COM. SECRETARY)
              With your permission ma'am, I'll
              start talking to the networks.

                         KIRBY
              Do it ! Lets get moving ladies and
              gentlemen, we all have a lot to
              accomplish.

The meeting breaks up and everyone makes for the
bathroom and shouts of **DIBS** are heard.

28 INT. NASA NEAR EARTH OBJECT PROGRAM HDQTRS — DAY 28

Five days have passed since the gifts were...(CONT'D)

delivered. Several attempts have been made to contact
VO again without success and the world is about to be
tipped on its ear...**again. MARIA COLE,** N.E.O. Director
is about to get the shock of her life. Co-director **JAY
PARKESHMUSHMUNDAR,** J.P. For short, comes in.

                    MARIA
          Hey J.P., whats the word ?

                    J.P.
          If you know any please save our
          butts prayers, say em quick !

                    MARIA
          Man, I haven't seen you this upset
          since your vasectomy.

                    J.P.
          Pull up your orbital data for the
          last twenty four hours, **hurry.**

                    MARIA
          Oooh...k

Maria taps on her console. Up pops the Near Earth
Asteroids Heliocentric Elliptic Orbital Elements data.
The list of current positions for all seven thousand
four hundred and forty one known near earth asteroids
and their orbital stats. The news is not good.

                    MARIA
          This can't be correct. This says
          they have all changed course.

                    J.P.
          That's not the bad news. I already
          ran the simulator with the altered
          trajectories.

                    MARIA
          And ?

                    J.P.
          They are all headed straight for
          us.

                    MARIA
          No way.

                    J.P.
          Yes way !

                         MARIA
          We've got to confirm this. Get a
          query off to the observatories.

                         J.P.
          If this info is correct, we are
          seriously screwed.

                         MARIA
          Maybe it's a Mr. VO thing. Maybe
          the White House already knows.

                         J.P.
          Elaine Kellog just left a message.
          Something about an advisory team ?

                         MARIA
          Let's see what she knows.
          (dialing) Hi Elaine, you called ?

                         ELAINE (V.O.)
          Hi Maria, the President wants me
          to put together a group that can
          advise the U.N. on using the VO
          technology. Interested ?

                         MARIA
          If my data is correct, we may not
          get the chance.

                         ELAINE (V.O.)
          What's going on ?

                         MARIA
          Every near earth asteroid we know
          of is heading for this planet.

                         ELAINE (V.O.)
          What...you're kidding right. How
          probable is that even ?

                         MARIA (ONE BREATH)
          About as probable as finding out
          there was an alien that loves
          cheese steaks living at the bottom
          of the Marianas trench and we
          would all be wearing glowing
          polygons on our foreheads and
          spending the rest of our lives on
          the toilet. About **that** probable !

                        ELAINE (V.O.)
OH.

                        MARIA
I was hoping it was a Mr. VO thing
and you already knew.

                        ELAINE (V.O.)
No clue I'm afraid. I'll try and
find out but Mr. VO isn't picking
up the phone at the moment.

                        MARIA
I'll confirm the data but it's
looking like brown trouser time.

                        ELAINE (V.O.)
Look, get back to me with a
confirmation and I'll talk to the
President. (clicks off)

                        MARIA
C'mon J.P., we have calls to make.

29 INT. VO SHIP GREAT ROOM - SIMULTANEOUS WITH 28   29

Ah, peace and quiet. VO is in the great room, sleeping
in his recliner surrounded by floating T'AH and it
seems as if they are trying to rouse him. All of the
polygonal screens are lit up with asteroid orbital
representations, thousands of them. An alarm is going
off but VO seems oblivious to the mayhem.

30 INT. WHITE HOUSE COMMUNICATIONS CENTER - DAY   30

Kirby is in the communications center working with
Laynie VAL.

                        LAYNIE
We've tried everything we could
think of chief. He either can't
hear us or doesn't want to talk.

                        KIRBY
What if we called Bill Duggin at
the BBC. He might have better
luck. Think you can get him on the
line for me ?

                        LAYNIE
Let's find out. (Dialing)

                    BBC CENTER LONDON (V.O.)
          Welcome to the BBC, how may I
          direct your call ?

                    LAYNIE
          This is the White House
          communications center. The
          President would like to speak with
          Mr. Duggin, is he available ?

                    BBC CENTER LONDON (V.O.)
          Yes ma'am, right away. Hold please.

                    BILL DUGGIN
          Madam President, I am honored. How
          may the BBC be of service to our
          U.S. neighbors.

                    KIRBY
          Mr. Duggin, we have been trying,
          without success, to contact Mr.
          VO. It is imperative that we speak
          with him ASAP, could you help ?

                    BILL DUGGIN (V.O.)
          Let me guess, asteroids ?

                    KIRBY
          How did you know ?

                    BILL DUGGIN (V.O.)
          We just got a report from one of
          our field correspondents doing
          background on the CHANDRA mission
          at NASA. It's all they are talking
          about. The BBC is at your service
          ma'am. I will try without delay
          and get back to you.

                    KIRBY
          Your assistance is greatly
          appreciated sir. (clicks off)

                    LAYNIE (TO KIRBY)
          You still want time on the
          networks tonight chief ?

                    KIRBY
          Yes, let's say eight o'clock. Tell
          them it's a National...(CONT'D)

                          KIRBY (CONT'D)
          Security broadcast and if they
          bitch about it remind them that
          the F in FCC means **Federal**.

                          LAYNIE
          Gotcha chief.

                          KIRBY
          I'll be in my office LAYNIE, call
          me the second you get any news.

Kirby walks out and heads quickly towards the Oval
Office to write her address to the nation.

31 <u>INT. VO SHIP GREAT ROOM - SEVERAL HOURS LATER</u>   31

Several screens have been receiving a broadcast from
Bill Duggin but VO is still sleeping soundly. The T'AH
are now mobbing his recliner, trying to get his
attention. He finally begins to stir.

                          BILL (ON SCREEN)
          Repeat, this is William Duggin of
          the BBC calling Mr. VO. Please
          come in sir, urgent.

VO yawns and stretches, waving away the swarming T'AH
and answers the call.

                          VO
               (blinking-sleepy)
          Hey BILL, how's your day going ?

                          BILL (ON SCREEN)
          Mr. VO, thank god I got hold of
          you. Are you responsible for what
          is happening in space.

                          VO
          Everything or something specific ?

                          BILL (ON SCREEN)
          Over seven thousand asteroids are
          headed straight for us !

                          VO
          OH.

                          BILL (ON SCREEN)
          What does that mean, oh ?

> VO
> I mean oh, like I didn't know oh.

> BILL (ON SCREEN)
> President Shirrah asked me
> personally to contact you. Is
> there anything you can tell me ?

> VO
> Nope. I guess I better see what's
> going on. Thanks for the heads up,
> I'll call you back... (clicks off)

VO looks intently at all of the monitors, the T'AH
constantly changing views of the incoming objects.

> VO
> Mmmmm, that's not good.

VO motions and the T'AH change screen views again to
the orbiting shell.

> VO
> Mmmmm.

32 <u>INT. WHITE HOUSE BROADCAST CENTER - NEAR 8 PM</u>   32

President Shirrah is almost ready for her broadcast to
the nation and Laynie Val runs in with news from Bill
Duggin.

> LAYNIE
> Chief, I got a call from Bill
> Duggin. He spoke to Mr. VO.

> KIRBY
> And ?

> LAYNIE
> Mr. VO said he wasn't aware but
> will investigate and call back.

> KIRBY
> Crap. I could have used better
> news. Thanks Laynie, let me know
> as soon as you get any more info.

> LAYNIE
> I'll stay on top of it chief.

Kirby moves to the podium with her notes. The crew
gives her the countdown to air.

> KIRBY
> My fellow Americans and citizens
> of the world, as you may know from
> some earlier telecasts today, a
> large number of near earth
> asteroids are heading this way.
> Current technology does not give
> us the ability to deal with this
> many objects at once. We have
> therefore contacted Mr. VO in the
> hope that our new benefactor may
> be able to help. He was contacted
> just hours ago and is looking into
> the situation. I urge you to
> remain calm, as the nearest of
> these objects is still several
> days away. Rest assured that every
> conceivable option will be
> explored and this office will
> broadcast updates as soon as they
> are available. Good night.

Lots of shocked expressions around the room and Kirby
gets jumped by the press corp.

> KIRBY (WAVES OFF)
> Sorry folks, no questions at this
> time, thank you.

33 EXT. VAR. WORLDWIDE - ALL ZONES - 2 DAYS LATER   33

Something is growing around the world. A montage of
locations, playgrounds, parking lots, courtyards,
parks, the lobbies of large buildings, anywhere there
is room for people to gather show strange objects,
made of polygons, springing up. Each has a 15 foot
central pillar surrounded by smaller spikes, like
cypress knees and are tipped with what look like
computer touch screens. Definitely VO-ish but not
glowing like everything else Mr. VO seems to do. A few
people can't resist touching the objects but they are
not functional...yet.

34 EXT. PACIFIC - 72 HOURS BEFORE 1ST IMPACT - DAY   34

A glowing transparent sphere, 20 feet across breaks
the surface over the Marianas trench and is...(CONT'D)

immediately picked up on satellite. The news is
quickly relayed around the world.

VO is sitting in the center of the craft but it is
simply hovering several feet above the sea where it
remains for the next two hours, then suddenly it
shoots straight up. Twenty miles, sixty miles, up and
out of the atmosphere, out and through the shell on an
intercept course with the largest, closest asteroid,
at unbelievable speed. NASA is watching it all.

Re-tasked, the Hubble is trained on the closest target
and has a perfect view of VO's arrival. Ben Darius and
Maria Cole are watching intently as VO's ship comes
along side and stabilizes the asteroid.

> BEN
> Man he got there fast. Close to
> light speed, remarkable.

> MARIA
> It stopped tumbling.

> BEN
> Has the trajectory changed any ?

Maria glances at another console

> MARIA
> Nothing yet....Wait, its speeding
> up. **They're both speeding up** !

Ben goes over to the same console

> BEN
> How fast ? Jeez, at this rate it
> will be here in a couple hours.

> MARIA
> Its like he is accelerating it on
> purpose. **What the hell man** ?

VO's ship separates from the asteroid and speeds ahead
back to earth, an estimated ten minutes ahead of the
recalculated impact. Right as VO's ship re-enters the
atmosphere an enormous polygonal tube breaks the
surface in the mid Atlantic ocean. One mile in
diameter, it climbs out to the orbiting shell and
attaches to a single large polygon precisely at the
expected entry point of the incoming asteroid. With no
warning and little time to even...(CONT'D)

panic, all the planet can do is hold its breath, wait
and pray.

                    BEN
          Here it comes.

                    MARIA
          It was nice knowing you Ben.

                    BEN
          You're not helping any.

The giant boulder screams into the shell and streaks
down the tube which constricts and stops it dead
exactly one mile above the sea. Several tense minutes
pass without incident.

                    MARIA
          What just happened ?

                    BEN
          I don't know but we're still here.

VO's ship is moving rapidly towards Washington D.C.
where it lands minutes later on the White House lawn.
Kirby and half the White House come running out to
meet the ship. It opens and VO steps out just as the
President nears.

                    VO
          Hi Kirby.

Kirby runs over and plants a relieved hug on VO.

                    KIRBY
          You could have let us know what
          you were up to ya know. A lot of
          people down here were panicked out
          of their minds.

                    VO
          Sorry Kirby, it was kinda my fault
          to begin with.

                    KIRBY
          What happened ?

                    VO
          I forgot to shut a light off.

                              KIRBY
          Must have been some light.

                              VO
          Yeah, my bad.

                              KIRBY
          I forgot in all the excitement,
          what about the rest of the
          asteroids ?

                              VO
          All taken care of Kirby. I'm
          sending the T'AH to gather them up
          for a soft landing on the moon.

                              KIRBY
          Why the moon ? Can't you just stop
          them or send them elsewhere ?

                              VO
          It's a surprise.

                              KIRBY
          Every time you say that I develop
          a migraine.

                              VO
          That's the spirit.

                              KIRBY
          Stop saying that and I'll buy you
          lunch.

                              VO
          Great. Hey, I hear the Pentagon
          has a Subway.

                              KIRBY
          I think the United States
          government can be a little more
          appreciative than that.

                              VO
          After you Kirby.

The President and VO walk towards the White House and
an improvised state dinner, while behind them, a group
of touch pad spikes leaps from the ground. Part of the
crowd notices and rushes back to get a closer look.
Kirby grabs VO by the arm.

                          KIRBY
               What the hell are those things Mr.
               VO ?

                          VO
               Prototypes, not hooked up yet. I
               had to work out a new travel
               system for you guys because I need
               to cannibalize a lot of your
               existing infrastructure for the
               power net.

                          KIRBY
               Couldn't you ask, just once.

                          VO
               No worries Kirby.

                          KIRBY
               Oi !

                          VO
               What exactly does that mean ?

                          KIRBY
               Its Jewish for I need a doughnut.

                          VO
               You're having the time of your
               life, admit it.

                          KIRBY
               You're not boring, that's for
               sure. Lets go eat, I think my
               sugar is low.

Kirby takes Mr. VO's arm and they head into the White
House. Although the security folks are trying to keep
order, its proving to be nearly impossible. All of the
major networks are now on the scene and clamoring for
access. As Mr. VO and Kirby sit down in the dining
room, he makes a suggestion.

                          VO
               You know Kirby, it's getting a
               little crowded in here. Let's give
               everybody something to do.

                          KIRBY
               Like what for instance ?

Unknown to Kirby, the tube that captured the asteroid
is just then swallowing it whole and converting the
material for use by the network.

> VO
> I just got a signal that the iron
> asteroid I captured is processed.
> There is a button on my ship that
> needs pushed. Let's let someone
> from the White House do it on
> camera.

> KIRBY
> If you're sure they can't screw it
> up, it's alright with me.

> VO
> Great. How about Elaine ?

> KIRBY
> (excited yell)
> Boy, would she love that. Run out
> and find Elaine Kellog and bring
> her back here.

> ELAINE (SHOUTS FROM DOOR)
> I'm out here chief, hang on.

Elaine pushes her way over to Kirby and VO escorted by
two security men.

> VO
> Hi Elaine, want to have a little
> fun ?

> ELAINE
> (very excited)
> I'm ready man. What can I do ?

> KIRBY
> We're going to have everyone
> follow you out to Mr. VO's ship.
> He needs you to push a button and
> the press can film it.

> ELAINE
> What's the button do ?

> VO
> Be surprised.

                         ELAINE
               The last time you said that the
               world got an enema.

                         VO
               Courage Camille.

                         KIRBY (TO SECURITY)
               Give us a walkie talkie and Elaine
               a headset. Mr. VO can talk her
               through it.

          Security hands out the necessary gear and motions
          everyone for an equipment check.

                         ELAINE
               Testing one, two, three testing.

                         VO
               Loud and clear Elaine. Go ahead
               out to the ship and I'll tell you
               what to do.

                         ELAINE
               Way cool.

          Kirby makes an announcement to the assembled crowd.

                         KIRBY
               Folks, my science adviser Elaine
               Kellog is going out to Mr. VO's
               ship to give him some assistance.
               You are all invited outside to
               observe and film.

          Several security flank VO and the President while the
          rest usher Elaine and the others out to the ship.
          Elaine approaches the sphere and calls VO.

                         ELAINE
               I'm at the ship. What now ?

                         VO (V.O.)
               First, go ahead in and sit down.

                         ELAINE
               I'm in. Next ?

                         VO (V.O.)
               There is a small console...(CONT'D)

                         VO (CONT'D)(V.O.)
in front of you with several
polygonal view screens. On the
large central screen there should
be a picture of the big tube I
used to catch the asteroid.

                         ELAINE
I see the tube but the asteroid is
gone. I hope that's a good thing.

                         VO (V.O.)
Good, good, good. Now, on the
bottom right of the console is a
large button.

                         ELAINE
I see it.

                         VO (V.O.)
Is it glowing ?

                         ELAINE
Yes.

                         VO (V.O.)
What color ?

                         ELAINE
Mauve.

                         VO (V.O.)
What the hell color is that ?

                         ELAINE
Like a light muted red.

                         VO (V.O.)
Gotcha, alright skip that button.
In the top center screen is a
picture of the T'AH inside my ship.

                         ELAINE
I see them.

                         VO (V.O.)
What are they doing ?

                         ELAINE
Not much. They're just floating
around.

                         VO (V.O.)
               Touch the center of the screen and
               say **now.**

                         ELAINE (TOUCHES SCREEN)
          Now.

The T'AH scatter to various screens in the ships great
room.

                         VO (V.O.)
               What color is the large button on
               the bottom right now ?

                         ELAINE
               I'm not sure, kinda aquamarine.

                         VO (V.O.)
               Anybody got a color chart, she's
               killing me.

                         KIRBY (V.O. BACK GROUND)
               Blue green Mr. VO.

                         VO (V.O.)
               Oh...push it.

                         ELAINE
               Done. Now what ?

                         VO (V.O.)
               Watch the device cluster on the
               lawn.

A surge of energy engulfs the ship and the nearby
devices light up in flashing gold and silver light.

                         ELAINE
               They lit up like Christmas trees.

                         VO (V.O.)
               Fabulous. Get out of the ship and
               walk over to nearest screen.

Elaine makes her way cautiously towards the closest
spike. At the same time a polygonal screen appears in
the dining room, in front of VO and the President. The
picture showing is of Elaine moving towards the
cluster. The screen scans the dining room from top to
bottom.

                                    ELAINE
                    I'm there, what now ?

                                    VO (V.O.)
                    Think about the Presidential
                    dining room. A picture of it and a
                    series of equations will become
                    visible on the touch pad in front
                    of you. As soon as you see it, put
                    both your hands flat on the pad.

                                    ELAINE
                    Got it.

Elaine closes her eyes and concentrates. The dining
room and several equations pop up.

                                    ELAINE
                    I see it, I see it.

Elaine touches the pad and a narrow vertical light
pipe from the central pillar touches her. Elaine
instantly walks out through the dining room screen.

                                    VO
                    Great, it works.

                                    KIRBY
                        (irked)
                    You mean you didn't know if it
                    worked or not ?

                                    VO
                        (Smiling)
                    How do you feel Elaine.

Elaine swoons, a bit dizzy.

                                    ELAINE
                    Wow. That was...**wow**.

                                    VO
                    Like going down a sink drain ?

                                    ELAINE
                    Yeah, that's exactly what I was
                    thinking.

                                    VO
                    Want to try it again ?

                        ELAINE
          Let the President have a turn.

                        VO
          Your turn Kirby.

                        KIRBY
          You'll owe me a doughnut.

                        VO
          Blaze a trail Kirby, I'll get you
          a bakers dozen.

                        KIRBY
          What do I do ?

                        VO
          This doorway is still connected to
          the gate Elaine used, just walk
          through and you will come out
          where she started.

                        KIRBY
          Here goes.

Kirby walks into the doorway and is squeezed out the
central pillar light pipe onto the lawn. A cheer goes
up from the crowd as Kirby, dizzy but unbroken, takes
a deep bow. Kirby walks back into the White House to
rejoin Elaine and VO.

                        KIRBY
          Now I know how a sausage feels.

An aid hands a note to Elaine.

                        ELAINE
          Chief, Ben Darius from NASA just
          called. He says the big tube that
          captured the asteroid has dropped
          back into the ocean and a new tube
          is spitting out thousands of
          objects headed out into space.

                        KIRBY
          Mr. VO ?

                        VO
          The T'AH are going to intercept
          the rest of the asteroids.

                         KIRBY
          You still going to take them to
          the moon ?

                         VO
          Yup.

                         ELAINE
          Why the moon ?

                         KIRBY (SHAKES HEAD)
          Don't ask.

Kirby moves over to sit next to VO.

                         KIRBY
          I am going to make a speech at the
          U.N., I'd like you to come too.

                         VO
          And do what, pray tell ?

                         KIRBY
          Maybe you could field a couple
          questions like the BBC interview ?

                         VO
          Sure, call me when you're ready.

                         KIRBY
          Done.

                         VO
          In the mean time, I better put
          some instructions on the travel
          pads before they go online or
          everyone will end up in your
          dining room. Goodnight ladies.

VO walks through the screen in the dining room and
reappears in his small ship on the lawn. As he lifts
off, the dining room doorway disappears.

                         ELAINE
          We never did eat Kirby, I'm
          starving.

                         KIRBY
          Let's get back to the office and
          I'll have something brought in. It
          could be a long night.

VO is programming the travel pads from the ships great
room. A representation of a pad is on the large
monitor in front of him. First, the instructions
appear in whatever language or dialect they speak.
Second, it then scans their polygon for the quantum
signature and third, displays a directory of terminal
locations and choices based on what the individual is
thinking. Touch the pad and you are off to virtually
anywhere. One of the wall screens is showing news
programs and a CNN report comes on.

> **JEAN FOLEY** - CNN
> After the fantastic film we all
> were treated to yesterday at the
> U.S. Capitol, people everywhere
> are eager to try the new travel
> system provided by Mr. VO.
> Unfortunately it seems to require
> some practice as a 12 year old
> girl from Boston discovered this
> morning. **JIM HALEY** reports...

> JIM
> I'm here with young **ABIGAIL SMITH**
> who got more than she bargained
> for when she decided to use the VO
> technology to visit her aunt in
> London, Ohio. Abigail, what
> happened ?

> ABIGAIL
> Well I was thinking of my aunts'
> house and I guess I wasn't
> watching the screen for the
> picture like your supposed to and
> when I touched the pad I ended up
> in London England.

> JIM
> How did you figure out that you
> were in England ?

> ABIGAIL
> No one talks like that in Ohio.

> JIM
> What did you do then ?

> ABIGAIL
> Some nice English people bought me
> lunch and helped me get back.

                         JIM
          Sounds like you had quite an
          adventure. Do you think you will
          try it again ?

                       ABIGAIL
          Oh sure, the nice English people
          said I should visit again but I
          think I'll take my mom next time.

                         JIM
          Well there you have it Jean, safe
          and sound but watch the picture on
          the pad. You may end up somewhere
          you didn't count on.

                         JEAN
          Thank you Jim and remember folks,
          no one can be mean anymore so
          travel is safer than ever. (screen
          clicks off)

36 <u>INT. OFFICE - BUSINESS THINK TANK - DAY</u>   36

Business forces are beginning to mobilize to study the
economic repercussions and possible opportunities
stemming from the VO technology.

                  KARL POTTS - FINANCIER
          Ladies and gentlemen, we need to
          start looking ahead.

                  ANNIE ROADS - BANKER
          I have already been looking at
          installing ATM terminals at these
          travel device locations.

                  REBECCA KOLE - DEVELOPER
          We will need more than that Annie.
          People will want services when
          they travel just like at airports,
          train and bus terminals.
          Restrooms, restaurants, shops with
          hug-able VO dolls for the kids,
          the works.

                       KARL POTTS
          We will have to move quickly.
          These things will put the public
          transportation industry out of
          business in a hurry.

                         RICHARD SCHIFF – AIRLINE EXEC
From what we've seen so far, these
devices are only intended to move
people and not cargo. We have time
to plan for a switch to air
freight when the bottom drops out
on passenger flights.

                      KARL
Everyone try to line up all the
capitol and support you can. We'll
meet back here next quarter.

As the meeting adjourns, 100 foot wide horizontal
polygons start appearing on open ground, in every
population center in the world. They have the words
"THROW IT IN HERE" showing across the front.

37 <u>INT. NASA – OFFICE OF BEN DARIUS – DAY</u>   37

A doorway appears in the office of Ben Darius and VO
steps out.

                      VO
Hi Ben, you busy ?

                      BEN
Does anybody ever get used to you
doing that ?

                      VO
Doesn't seem to bother Kirby
anymore so there is probably hope
for you. Say Ben, NASA have any
plans to go back to the moon ?

                      BEN
Eventually, I hope. Why ?

                      VO
I need to go this week, want to
come along ?

                      BEN
Yes...yes I would, very much.

                      VO
The T'AH are delivering the rest
of the asteroids to the moon. They
will arrive in two days. I want to
be there to see it first hand.

                           BEN
          The impacts could be catastrophic.
          It's whole orbit could shift.

                           VO
          It's okay Ben, they're soft
          landing them all. Suggestions on
          where ?

                           BEN
          I like Mare Humorum myself.

                           VO
          Done. Do you want them in a pile,
          laid out flat or maybe a big
          smiley face for the kids ?

                           BEN
          I've never had this much fun in my
          life. How will we get there ? A
          small ship like the one you used
          the other day ?

                           VO
          Not enough room. You'll want to
          bring a couple people and some
          equipment. We could just drive
          there. Got anything we can use ?

                           BEN
          There is a prototype buggy we have
          been testing in New Mexico. It's a
          habitat on wheels that holds six,
          looks kinda like a big bug.

                           VO
          Super. I will have the T'AH level
          a site at Mare Humorum. Now, I
          need you to take this with you to
          New Mexico.

VO produces a sphere that looks like a miniature
soccer ball, except it glows of course.

                           BEN
          What's this for ?

                           VO
          Quantum ball. The network is busy
          with other stuff at the moment so
          I can't scan the New...(CONT'D)

                         VO (CONT'D)
            Mexico site or the moon from
            orbit. This will scan your
            location. The T'AH will deliver an
            identical ball to Mare Humorum so
            we can link with the moon. Cool ?

                         BEN
            To quote my Jamaican friends,
            Massive Cool !

                         VO
            See you in two days Ben.

VO walks through the doorway and blinks out.

                         BEN
            What a day.

38 INT. VO SHIP - LATER SAME DAY   38

VO is receiving a call from Bill Duggin at the BBC.

                         BILL DUGGIN (ON SCREEN)
            William Duggin calling for Mr. VO,
            come in please.

                         VO
            Hi BILL, what can I do for you ?

                         BILL DUGGIN (ON SCREEN)
            The President just called. The
            meeting at the U.N. is set for
            tomorrow morning at nine. Can you
            be there ?

                         VO
            Hang on just a sec Bill, I'm
            working on something for NASA.

VO motions to one of the T'AH who comes down and takes
in a quantum ball for the moon. VO motions again and
the T'AH exits the same tube used by the others to
head into space. VO turns his attention back to Bill
Duggin.

                         VO
            All done Bill.

                         BILL DUGGIN (ON SCREEN)
            May I ask with what ?

                              VO
          I'm taking a NASA team to the moon
          in two days to watch the T'AH
          deliver the rest of the asteroids.

                         BILL (ON SCREEN)
          Any chance the BBC can tag along ?

                              VO
          Sorry Bill, not this trip. Don't
          worry, there will be other trips
          and you're next, I promise.

                         BILL (ON SCREEN)
          I appreciate that.

                              VO
          I have an exclusive for you
          anyway. I was saving it for a
          surprise but since you asked.

VO motions to the T'AH who activate a large screen. A
view of space appears with the moon dead center.

                         BILL (ON SCREEN)
          What am I seeing ?

                              VO
          One of the T'AH is taking a
          quantum beacon to the moon in
          preparation for our trip to Mare
          Humorum. You will see it delivered
          and the doorway form. Fair enough ?

                         BILL (ON SCREEN)
          By god Mr. VO, you're a man after
          my own heart. Thank you.

                              VO
          Anything for my friends at the
          BBC. Tell you what, as a bonus I
          will have this T'AH stay in orbit
          to broadcast live pictures of the
          main event.

                         BILL (ON SCREEN)
          What a thrill for our viewers.

                              VO
          Two days Bill, don't forget.
          (clicks off)

VO settles in to watch world events from the comfort of his recliner. Busy T'AH constantly tend the hundreds of instruments and monitors.

> VO
> Well, so far, so good.

39 <u>INT. UNITED NATIONS - NEXT DAY - 9 AM</u>   39

President Shirrah is preparing to address the U.N. Assembly, hopefully with Mr. VO but he never told Bill Duggin whether he was coming or not. U.N. Secretary General, **CAI MORWEN**, talks to Kirby before the session.

> CAI
> Hi Kirby, you ready to go ?

> KIRBY
> Yes but our friend Mr. VO isn't here yet.

> CAI
> I was looking forward to meeting that person.

> KIRBY
> He is something.

> CAI
> I guess we should get started.

The two women walk out to the assembly floor and CAI opens the session.

> CAI
> Ladies and gentlemen of the United Nations, thank you all for attending this unique session. Our organization was formed as a bulwark in support of civilization at times of societal stress and change. Never could we conceive of the extraordinary events of the past few weeks. Finding that we have a galactic neighbor residing within our own planet, the amazing gifts we now enjoy that have allowed the lame to walk, the blind to see and eliminate hunger. A wealth of benefits to humanity beyond our ability to...(CONT'D)

                         CAI (CONT'D)
          repay. And this selfless
          individual continues to...

A polygonal doorway springs up on the assembly floor
and VO steps out.

                         VO
          Hi folks, sorry I'm late.

Spontaneous applause erupts in the hall and continues
unabated for several minutes. VO walks around the
chamber shaking hands, smiling and laughing with the
delegates. Finally he lopes up to the podium and
greets Cai Morwen who is flanked by President Shirrah.

                         CAI
          Mr. VO, welcome to the United
          Nations.

                         VO
          Thanks Cai, glad to be here. I
          love your suit, Armani ?

                         CAI
          No sir, Jacque-Pen-Yea, D street.

                         VO
          Thrifty, I like it.

                         CAI
          Madam President, would you do the
          introduction please.

Kirby shakes hands with Cai and VO and takes the
podium.

                         KIRBY
          Ladies and gentlemen, Madam
          Secretary, citizens of the world,
          it is my great honor to introduce
          the person who has done more for
          humanity in a month than we have
          collectively accomplished in the
          last ten thousand years, please
          welcome Mr. VO.

Another round of applause. Kirby steps aside and VO
speaks to the assembly.

                         VO
          First of all, I'd like to thank
          Kirby for being so patient with
          me. I've dropped some real
          shockers on her and she took it
          all with tremendous grace. As you
          are all aware by now, I have used
          some of your resources to repair
          my ship and in return for your
          generosity, I am using some of my
          technology to help out a little. I
          hope everyone is enjoying their
          gifts, sorry for the number of
          bathroom breaks but that will
          taper off...**eventually**. I have
          laid out the beginnings of your
          new transportation system, the
          same system you saw Kirby and
          Elaine Kellog use on TV.

                         KIRBY
          I'm still dizzy.

                         VO
          You're a good sport Kirby.

Scattered laughter and applause.

                         VO (CONT'D)
          I still have a few more surprises
          for you. I just set up your new
          recycling system in all of the
          major population centers and it
          will be operational in a few
          hours. Its pretty simple, if you
          don't need or want it, throw it
          in. The network will instantly
          reprocess it into usable energy
          with zero waste. What else...I'm
          taking some NASA guys to the moon
          tomorrow, you'll want to watch
          that. Let's see, what else, the
          shell that orbits the earth now is
          collecting energy from space and
          storing it in my ship in the
          Marianas. I am working on a way to
          get all of that free energy to
          everyone but I haven't worked that
          one out yet. Also, I hope you are
          all making an extra special effort
          at...(CONT'D)

                              VO (CONT'D)
          niceness. You've all seen the
          stories on the news about what
          happens to mean people. Just
          remember, these things you're
          getting are only tools. What
          happens afterwards is entirely up
          to you and just FYI, humans are at
          least as smart as anyone else my
          race knows, not as well adjusted
          as some but smart enough. That's
          it for today folks. Thank you very
          much for your kind welcome and
          warm wishes.

VO walks to the doorway amid deafening applause and a
standing ovation, waves, smiles and exits in a blink.

40 <u>INT. VO SHIP LABORATORY - LATER SAME DAY</u>   40

VO is in his ships laboratory where he is trying to
work out the power distribution problem.

                              VO
          Mmmmm, what to do, what to do ?

Uncertain how to proceed VO does whatever any person
with time on his hands and a computer does, he surfs
the internet. Motioning to the T'AH, they manipulate
the many view screens and bring up site after site on
electricity. Franklin, Edison, Westinghouse then
finally Nikola Tesla and a flash of inspiration.

                              VO
          Mmmmm, Tesla.

VO manipulates instruments in the lab walls. A
computer generated image materializes within a group
of floating T'AH. Nothing extraordinary, by appearance
just a smooth red ball, shooter marble size.

                              VO
     Mmmmm.

VO taps a few times on a control pad and the T'AH
immediately go to work. More lights come on revealing
an elongated space many stories high. T'AH are forming
row after row of gigantic clear holding tanks with a
large red polygon over top of each. VO strikes the
control pad again and a few red marbles...(CONT'D)

begin to ooze out and drop into the tanks, then
hundreds, thousands, tens of thousands, millions upon
millions until, finally, it slows to a trickle and
stops. A number pops up on the main view screen.
Exactly one billion.

                    VO
          That should be plenty for now. I
          need Bill.

VO makes his way to the great room, motions to the
T'AH and transmits. His picture pops up on monitors
all over the BBC building.

                    VO
          Hi BBC, this is VO. I'd like to
          speak with Bill Duggin please.

                    A BBC TECHNICIAN (V.O.)
          I will check for you right away
          sir (Yells out) Get Mr. Duggin on
          a mic quick, tell him its Mr. VO.

Bill was watching and is already running for a studio.
He rushes into the nearest booth and grabs a headset.

                    BILL
          Hello..hello ?

                    VO
          Hi Bill, your viewers digging that
          moon shot ?

                    BILL
          Yes sir. Our world audience has
          tripled, many thanks.

                    VO
          Wait till they see the NASA trip.

                    BILL
          We're ready. Is that why you
          called ?

                    VO
          No, I need a favor Bill. Is your
          invite to come back still good ?

                    BILL
          Absolutely, how can I help ?

                              VO
          During the moon thing, I want to
          do a little demonstration at your
          studios.

                              BILL
          During ? You said you were going
          with the NASA team to the moon.

                              VO
          One of me is.

                              BILL
          Splendid. Where do you want to set
          up ? How much space will you need ?

                              VO
          I think I have most of your energy
          problem solved. I want to set up
          cameras at your buildings main
          power boxes. Can you do that for
          me ?

                              BILL
          Certainly, certainly. I'll get
          started right away. What time ?

                              VO
          The NASA guys and I are leaving
          New Mexico at six AM tomorrow, so
          let's say two PM your time.

                              BILL
          That works for me Mr. VO.

                              VO
          Great, see you then. (Clicks off)

VO now calls Ben Darius's cell phone. Ben is already
on site in New Mexico with the NASA team.

                         BEN (ON SCREEN)
          Hello ?

                         VO (V.O.)
          Hi Ben, everybody excited ?

                              BEN
          You bet. The best space people on
          earth are here and ready for the
          experience of a lifetime.

                              VO
          If this goes well, traveling to
          the moon will be like driving to
          the mall.

                              BEN
          I can't wait. Hey, want to see the
          buggy ?

Ben turns his phone around and the new crawler comes
into view. Looking like a scoop of ice cream on a
spiders back, the vehicle tows two work modules behind
connected together by flexible pressure tunnels. It
can hold two astronauts driving and up to six in the
other sections.

                              VO
          She's a beauty Ben. I need to
          program the quantum ball, where is
          the team ?

                              BEN
          They're all in the crawler doing
          safety checks. You need them ?

                              VO
          Not for this part. Hold the ball
          up to the camera.

Ben pulls the ball out of his pocket and holds it in
front of the lens. VO motions to the T'AH, one of whom
activates a large gauge. The ball glows silver, gold
and scans the entire area. At that moment, (inset) the
ball on Mare Humorum activates also.

                              VO
          We're good to go Ben. Tuck that
          ball into the lead module and I'll
          see you in the morning.

                              BEN
          Thanks again for the opportunity.
          (clicks off)

40 EXT. SPACE - SAME DAY   40

We see the T'AH in space, bringing in the asteroids
for a scheduled soft touch down, at seven AM Mountain
Time the following day, on Mare Humorum.

41 INT. BBC TELEVISION CENTER - SAME DAY   41

BBC technicians with Bill Duggin setting up by the
power boxes for the VO demo next day.

42 INT. VO SHIP - STORAGE AREA - SAME DAY   42

Thousands of T'AH are arranging the power marbles in
giant upside down pyramids ready for delivery. VO is
in the laboratory again working on the rest of the
delivery system. He works on a control pad, a burst of
energy flows out of the ship into the fourteen
vertical connectors. On each connector a large, dull
red ball, one mile in diameter forms at seventy eight
miles above sea level.

                         VO
              I need a break.

VO stretches out in his recliner.

43 INT. VO SHIP GREAT ROOM - NEXT MORNING - DAWN   43

VO 1 is already on the move through a doorway to meet
the NASA team in New Mexico. VO 2 is monitoring
countless screens, making final preparations for the
BBC broadcast, the asteroid landings on Mare Humorum
and the T'AH deliveries of the power marbles, if the
demo goes well.

44 EXT. NEW MEXICO - 6 AM   44

A doorway opens in the New Mexico desert at the NASA
test site and VO 1 steps into the morning sun. The
NASA team is under a canopy having breakfast.

                        VO 1
              Morning folks, beautiful day.

                        BEN
                   (walking over)
              Good morning Mr. VO, come on over
              and I'll introduce you to the team.

The entire group gets on its feet and walks out to
meet VO. Ben does the introductions as all shake hands.

                        BEN
              VO, this is **LINDA PAUL**, mission
              commander.

                        LINDA
              An honor to meet you sir.

                         BEN
          JOEL KRAUSE, our mechanical genius.

                         JOEL
          A genuine pleasure sir.

                         BEN
          SVETLANA KOBLIKOV, our
          distinguished Russian pilot.

                         SVETLANA
          I've dreamed of this moment my
          whole life Mr. VO.

                         VO 1
          You mean meeting an alien or going
          to the moon ?

                         SVETLANA
          Both sir, both.

                         BEN
          And last but not least, **LAKOTA
          HIGHTOWER** our mission generalist
          and cinematographer.

                         LAKOTA
          Pleased to meet you Mr. VO.

                         BEN
          That's the whole team Mr. VO and
          we're raring to go.

                         VO 1
          Great. Let me adjust this doorway
          a little bit and we'll get going.

VO walks to the doorway and touches the edge. It
expands large enough to handle the space buggy.

                         VO 1 (CONT'D)
          Saddle up.

Everyone dons their space suits before starting out.
VO's gloves have seven fingers, a gift from NASA. They
all pile into the buggy. Linda and Joel in the drive
section and the rest into the towed modules. The
crawler moves slowly forward, passes the threshold and
rolls out onto the plain at Mare Humorum.

As the astronauts E.V.A. to the surface, VO 2 is
leaving the ship for his trip to the BBC.

                    VO 1
          Get your gear set up Lakota, the
          asteroids will be arriving any
          minute now.

                    LAKOTA
          Right behind you Mr. VO.

Linda is in the driver position up front on the
crawler next to Joel.

                    LINDA
          Stay together everyone, I don't
          want to lose anybody.

                    VO 1
          Oh mom.

                    SVETLANA
          I swear, this has to be the most
          fun you can have standing up.

                    JOEL
          Hey Mr. VO, which way should we be
          looking ?

                    BEN
          Up man, up.

                    VO 1
               (Pointing up)
          They're coming.

Thousands of T'AH are bringing their asteroids down
slowly onto the plain north to south.

                    BEN
          What did you decide Mr. VO, lay
          flat or in a pile ?

                    LINDA
          You mean you guys **actually**
          discussed how to stack these
          boulders ?

                    BEN
          Is that cool or what !

The team is helping LAKOTA set up another camera to
catch different angles on the asteroid landings.

                    JOEL
        Mr. VO, aren't we a little close ?

                    VO 1
    Nah.

                    LINDA
        This is amazing !

The T'AH bring these rocky monsters, some more than a
mile across, down so gently, they hardly create a
ripple. Settling of their own weight like pushing your
fist into a sand pile. The drops, which began north of
the teams position, are coming closer. Uncomfortably
closer. The final asteroid drops just 50 yards away
and is so large it looks as if someone dropped a
mountain on the front porch. All of the T'AH, except
the one transmitting from orbit to the BBC, fly back
to earth to join the others for the distribution of
the power marbles.

                    SVETLANA
        Jeez, jumping g-men !

                    BEN
            (chuckles)
        Where did that come from ?

                    SVETLANA
        Old American gangster movies.

                    BEN
    Aah.

The remaining T'AH still transmitting live video from
orbit, sends new detailed views of Mare Humorum. The
astronauts pick up the feed on their helmet displays.

                    LINDA
            (amused)
        You've got to be kidding me !

                    LAKOTA
        O.M.G. !

                    JOEL
            (smiling)
        My mother would have loved it.

                          SVETLANA
              Suddenly I feel like buying the
              world a Coke.

BEN has broken into an unstoppable fit of laughter.

                          VO (TO BEN)
              Breathe man, breathe.

                          BEN
              Its brilliant, absolutely inspired.

The scene from orbit reveals a colossal peace sign in
the center of Mare Humorum. As the image races around
the world, great sustained cheers go up everywhere.

                          VO 1
              Well, I wish we had more time
              ladies and gentlemen but I need to
              get a few more things done today.

                          LINDA
              Shucks, I was hoping we'd have
              time to roam around a bit.

                          VO 1
              Another day Linda, I promise.

                          LINDA
              Well, let's pack up.

                          LAKOTA
              I got some fantastic footage.

                          SVETLANA (TO LAKOTA)
              Can you get me a copy for my
              daughter ? She loves this stuff.

                          LAKOTA
              Only if I get your autograph for
              my daughter.

                          SVETLANA
              Deal.

The team climbs into the rover and turns around to
head on back to Earth. The crawler glides effortlessly
through the doorway, back at the New Mexico site, safe
and sound.

                          VO 1
          Ben, keep that ball safe, you can
          reuse it for future trips.

                          BEN
          On behalf of the entire team and
          NASA Mr. VO, thank you.

All shake hands and part company. VO walks back
through the doorway and comes out in the great room of
the ship just after VO 2 leaves to join Bill at the
BBC. VO 1 motions to the T'AH and all the video
screens light up. An image of the vertical connectors
comes up and the once dull red spheres begin to glow
brightly and are now fully powered. VO 1 walks through
to the immense storage area with the stacked power
marbles, many thousands of T'AH hovering on standby.
VO 1 activates a large central monitor to observe the
BBC power test.

45 INT. BBC CENTER - LONDON - 2 PM LOCAL TIME   45

The cameras are ready, VO 2 is ready and Bill gives
the thumbs up to the crew.

                          BILL
          Good evening and welcome again to
          a special BBC event with our good
          friend from outer space, Mr. VO

                          VO 2
          Hi humanity. You're probably
          wondering why we are in the
          basement of BBC Center. Well, Bill
          and I are going to conduct a
          little test.

VO pulls a small glowing red marble from his pocket.

                          BILL
          I see you brought something new.

                          VO 2
          I have been working on a way to
          distribute all the free energy the
          orbiting shell captures and this
          is what I came up with.

                          BILL
          What is it ?

                          VO 2
          Its a receiver of sorts. My race
          doesn't use electricity so I
          wasn't sure what to do but I
          surfed your web and found the
          research of Nikola Tesla. I
          adapted one of his ideas to make
          this work. I have created large
          transmitters on the vertical
          strands that connect the shell in
          orbit to my ship. As you can see,
          this marble is glowing which means
          my counterpart has activated the
          network and we are ready to try it
          out. When I attach this device to
          your power box, it should begin
          receiving energy wirelessly from
          the transmitters and supply all of
          the electricity your building
          requires. At least that's what's
          supposed to happen.

                          BILL
          Wonderful.

                          VO 2
          It's wonderful if it works.

VO approaches the first and largest in a line of power
boxes.

                          VO 2
          Is this one the main guys ?

                        TECHNICIAN
          Yes sir.

                          VO 2
          You might want to back up a bit.

VO gingerly touches the marble to the box and
immediately a spider web of red filaments spreads out
from the ball to engulf the box and wiring. The large
cables coming into the box glow bright red and
disappear, all the way to the outside connection at
the street. The power stays on without a flicker.

                          VO 2 (TO BEN)
                       (very surprised)
          Great, no explosions or other
          assorted mayhem.

                    BILL
          Astounding. Where did the incoming
          wiring go ?

                    VO 2
          You don't need your connection to
          the power station anymore so the
          network recycled it. Your electric
          bill just dropped to zero.

                    BILL
          Not to be a wet blanket Mr. VO but
          what if this marble would fail ?
          Nothing lasts forever.

                    VO 2
          This will.

                    BILL
          But VO, for this to work we would
          need millions.

                    VO 2
          I figured about 1 billion to start
          off with. Once we see how it goes,
          we'll make sure everybody gets one.

                    BILL
          How long will it take to
          manufacture that many ?

                    VO 2
          Already done and they are ready
          for distribution. Instructions
          will be broadcast by the T'AH in
          the local language, as they are
          delivered.

                    BILL
          There you have it ladies and
          gentlemen. Just when you thought
          you had lost your marbles you get
          new ones. Please stand by for
          instructions from the T'AH on how
          to install your devices when they
          are delivered in your area. (Cut)

                    BILL (CONT'D)
          Are you going back to your ship or
          can you stay for supper ?

Bill and VO 2 walk towards the doorway.

> VO 2
> I hate to pass up a good cheese
> steak Bill but I gotta get back
> and spell my counterpart.

> BILL
> (shaking hands)
> Thank you again VO for allowing
> the BBC audience to share these
> unique experiences.

> VO 2
> No sweat Bill.

VO walks through the doorway and blinks out.

46 <u>INT. VO SHIP GREAT ROOM - SAME DAY</u>   46

VO2 appears in the great room and greets VO 1.

> VO 2
> Hi VO, everything ready ?

> VO 1
> Yup.

VO 2 disappears into a doorway. The remaining VO
studies the monitors showing the planned T'AH delivery
paths, to metropolitan centers, around the world. VO
settles into his recliner and calls the President.
Kirby is in the bath when her cell phone rings.

> KIRBY (ON SCREEN)
> (a trifle irked)
> **What** ?

> VO
> That looks fun, nice bubbles.

> KIRBY (ON SCREEN)
> You're killing me man.

> VO
> You still owe me dinner you know.

> KIRBY (ON SCREEN)
> **Now** ?

                         VO
          I've always wanted to try barbecue.

                         KIRBY (ON SCREEN)
          We can do that. How many people ?

                         VO
          Why don't you bring Elaine and
          Tom. I'll grab a few others and
          meet you on the front lawn, like
          five tomorrow ?

                         KIRBY (ON SCREEN)
          Done. What would you like to eat ?

                         VO
          Surprise me but no seafood.

                         KIRBY (ON SCREEN)
          Gotcha. I have to go, my waters
          getting cold.

                         VO
          Yeah, I can see that. Goodnight
          Kirby. (clicks off)

                         KIRBY
          I need a raise.

47 <u>EXT. WHITE HOUSE LAWN - AFTERNOON NEXT DAY</u>   47

The White House staff is deep into putting on the
barbecue for their guest of honor. The media is also
in attendance but remembering the previous dining room
fiasco, kept outside the fence this time. Its going to
be quite a party and a full moon to boot. As the clock
creeps towards five Kirby, Elaine, and a few others
are seated under a tent having drinks when fifteen
doors open all over the lawn. Out walks Carol Barr,
Beth Spall, Robert Carlisle, Admiral Tullie, Captain
Bradley, Odette Hume, Jane Colucci, Ben Darius, Bill
Duggin, Cai Morwen, Linda Paul, Joel Krause, Svetlana
Koblikov, Larota Hightower and VO himself. Everyone
waving to each other and shaking hands. A very happy
reunion. VO greets the crowd as they meet by the
President.

                         KIRBY
          Hi VO, the media is calling this
          group the VO-sters you know.

                         VO
          Catchy nickname. What's cooking
          Kirby ?

                         KIRBY
          Everything. If its grill-able,
          we're cooking it but no seafood as
          requested. What can I get for you ?

                         VO
          I'd love a root beer.

                         KIRBY
          Coming right up.

Kirby hands VO a cold bottle from the cooler and
everyone sits down to dinner, laughing and swapping
stories.

                         BEN
          Hey VO, how soon for the power
          devices to be delivered ?

                         VO
          They are already on their way Ben.
          In fact, the first wave should be
          hitting this area about now.

Everyone looks around and coming down Pennsylvania
avenue is a T'AH with what looks like a gigantic bunch
of grapes hanging underneath it. Instructions being
broadcast can be faintly heard as people run up to
pluck off their prize.

                         KIRBY
          I should grab one for the White
          House.

                         VO
          The more the merrier Kirby.

As darkness begins to fall Kirby and VO are sitting
together looking up at the moon and the peace sign.

                         KIRBY (BOTTLE RAISED)
          To peace in our time.

                         VO
          Well Kirby, its a start.

                         THE END

Made in the USA
Middletown, DE
09 December 2021

54808414R00066